FREAKY MONDAY

MARY RODGERS
· AND ·
HEATHER HACH

HARPER

An Imprint of HarperCollins*Publishers*

Freaky Monday
Copyright © 2009 by Mary Rodgers
All rights reserved. Printed in the United States of America. No part of
this book may be used or reproduced in any manner whatsoever without written permission except in the case of brief quotations embodied
in critical articles and reviews. For information address HarperCollins
Children's Books, a division of HarperCollins Publishers, 10 East 53rd
Street, New York, NY 10022.
www.harpercollinschildrens.com

Library of Congress Cataloging-in-Publication Data
Rodgers, Mary.
   Freaky Monday / Mary Rodgers and Heather Hach.—1st ed.
      p.   cm.
   Summary: Thirteen-year-old Hadley begins to better understand
her teacher and herself when she has to spend a day in her teacher's
body.
   ISBN 978-0-06-166481-6
   [1. Teacher-student relationships—Fiction. 2. Self-perception—
Fiction. 3. Schools—Fiction.] I. Hach, Heather. II. Title.
PZ7.R6155Frm 2009   2008044397
[Fic]—dc22   CIP
                                          AC

10   11   12   13   14   CG/CW   10 9 8 7 6 5 4 3 2 1
❖
First paperback edition, 2010

To Sophie and Clara
—M.R.

For Harper
—H.H.

FREAKY MONDAY

CHAPTER 1

I hate Mondays.

Okay, so it's not an original thought. So does most of the planet.

But seriously, I'm positively allergic and my soul breaks out into hives at the very thought. Mondays. It's like the February of days—no one likes it at all, and they should make every Monday shorter somehow, just like they had the good sense to make February the shortest month. (I'd suggest every Monday be fifteen hours, for example.)

I should back up first. I'm rambling and you have no idea who I am or why I hate Mondays or any of it. First off, I'm thirteen and my name is Hadley, which for years I thought sounded like a brand of car more than a human name, but I'm just now beginning to realize it may be cool. It's certainly not Jessica or Jennifer, though I'm sure those are two names that would make me instantly more popular.

And while we're on the topic of being instantly more popular, I should mention my older sister, Tatum. Even her name sounds exotic, huh? Tatums don't sweat or break out or still pathetically wear underwear with days of the week on them (unlike some people I know). Tatum's beauty is at once exotic and somehow all-American—a sort of teenage supermodel. If you walk down the beauty aisle of your local drugstore, you're bound to see Tatum-worthy beauties staring back at you from the shampoo bottles, giggling through a Photoshop-perfect smile. Tatum seriously has that shimmery rare prettiness that makes you instantly think Hair Commercial. And the irony is Tatum is actually the brunette and I'm the (mousy) blonde, yet *still* our fortunes could not be reversed. In movies, brunette is code for "friend" and blonde translates to "girlfriend." But this movie logic isn't my reality. Tatum's dark hair—even when thrown together in a sloppy updo—looks ravishing. My hair looks like burnt straw.

To make matters worse, Tatum's genuinely cool. Her musical taste runs more indie, not crappy bubble-gum stuff. *And* she's been volunteering with Habitat for Humanity since, like, the sixth grade. Seriously, she's a freak of nature—she looks like MTV but can talk like PBS. She's truly bright and creative and bubbles in a way

I'm never going to bubble. She's gifted in every arena known to mankind except one: academics. Math, more specifically. Seriously, her math abilities are somewhere on a par with Bubbles the chimp. Maybe she just doesn't apply herself (something I'll *never* have to grapple with— more on that in a second) . . . or maybe Tatum has some medical condition, a sort of math dyslexia or something. Who knows.

All I know is that it's impossible to hate Tatum, though lots of people have probably tried. And it would be easy to lump her into the Mean Girls category based upon appearance alone. Yet Tatum treats everyone really decently—that's her jujitsu offense. And it seems to work.

Tatum doesn't hate Mondays. They're "opportunities." Okay, she's never used that term, but she is an optimistic person, the make-lemonade-out-of-lemons sort of girl. Then again, I would be too, if Mom and Dad had passed along her DNA salad to me.

So back to this morning . . . at breakfast, which, for the record, I firmly believe should include coffee. I need some pep but Mom refuses to let me drink it. Like coffee's some adult mystery. And this wouldn't happen in France, incidentally. Drinking coffee—and no one's died of a coffee overdose, am I right?—would probably be encouraged, as would beret wearing and meaningful conversations. Anyway—I mentioned I ramble, right?—at breakfast, Tatum was eating her sensible all-the-food-groups-are-represented breakfast (she got the good metabolism, too), and Mom went ballistic on me for not feeding Higgins the cat or making my bed. She probably wanted to throw in a "Why can't you be more like your sister, Tatum?" but has watched enough *Oprah* to realize this is a bad idea. In protest, I snuck some of her coffee behind her back. And it was *not* decaf.

Before you think I'm really a Rebel Yell, defiant-fist-in-the-air sort of teenager, also consider that when a report aired this morning on the *Today* show about how an unusual comet got a wee bit too close to Earth for astronomers' comfort, I instantly Wikipedia-ed "comet" to find out exactly what a comet is in case it came up in a pop quiz in earth science. (If you're wondering, comets are small solar-system bodies that orbit the sun and, when close enough to the sun, exhibit a visible coma and/or tail.) Like I said, I apply myself way too hard and I'm a classic nerd. Even when I try to watch silly reality TV at night like a normal teenage girl should, I get itchy and nervous and have to dash to my room to go over my reading just one more time. Seriously, it's pathological.

At least I have a 4.3 GPA (because of all my extra-credit assignments, thank you very much) to show for it.

Back to my morning.

After all this comet-crash-studying and my mom's tirade, Tatum drove me to school. She always drops me off at junior high before she goes on to her high school. The drive is actually one of my favorite times of the day. We listen to NPR and talk like civilized adults. Being in the car with Tatum is almost like being in our own private world, safe from the nonsense. Tatum always makes me think I'm the only person in the world.

And our world—at least on paper—sounds cooler than it actually is. We live in San Marino, California, where occasionally movie crews come to film our quaint little town, trying to capture that slice of Americana that doesn't really exist except in the movies or on TV. I live there and I wish life was like a movie, let me tell you! Just because we're close to Los Angeles, don't think that I know Reese Witherspoon or anything. I wish. I don't shop at fancy boutiques or tan 24/7. I don't surf. And the only celebrity I've ever spoken to was the Quaker Oats guy. (Not that I knew his name off the bat. I Googled him when I got home, and within three clicks, I had my man.) We were both waiting at the same dentist's office reception area, and he was reading one of those women's magazines about sexy secrets (those are cool) and tasty new chicken recipes (those are not). He said to me while perusing some article, "It's about time she got a job." And I had zero idea who he was talking about or what the context was, but like I said, I recognized him from TV, so I nodded and said, "Yeah," and actually hoped he'd continue to talk to me. Then I realized he may have been slightly insane and no one would care that I had this big conversation with the guy who pitches oatmeal on TV. I was telling Tatum this story just the other day on our way to school and she guffawed . . . which made me feel great. I just love our time in the morning driving to school together.

But our sealed-off utopia always has to come to an end. She pulls up to my Burroughs Junior High and I can see these teenage dorks salivating at the sight of her. Her '93 Accord seriously causes the sea—or at least the parking lot—to part. Last year Eddie Potts actually asked me how Tatum could possibly be my sister. Maybe there was a mix-up at the hospital? Did your mom get remarried and THEN have you? Everyone died laughing and I felt my heart freeze-dry and shatter.

When I jump out of the car, Tatum always grabs my hand and gives it a little squeeze, telling me, "Have a great day, okay?" And I always respond back, "Ditto, kiddo." This whole exchange sounds sort of Mom, but it's actually quite nice. She also tells me to say hi to Ms. Pitt, my English teacher and her favorite junior high teacher. Tatum's always going on and on about how awesome Ms. Pitt is. And frankly, I fail to grasp the greatness of her. I mean, sure, she's not your average geriatric teacher and she drives a hybrid, but she's also a little . . . I don't know, self-help or something. Like that aunt who drinks too much wine at Thanksgiving and wants to "really talk" and all you want to do is proofread your English essay before school starts up again on Monday.

So Tatum and I said our good-byes and as I headed into school, watching the morons crane their necks and whisper about my goddess sister, it dawned on me.

IT WAS MONDAY.

MONDAY THE SIXTEENTH OF OCTOBER.

THE DAY I WAS SUPPOSED TO GIVE MY ORAL PRESENTATION ON *TO KILL A MOCKINGBIRD*.

From my use of ALL CAPS, I suppose you've jumped to the conclusion that I was not prepared. At all.

You see, I switched to a new Super Student Planner Plus last week, which is supposed to be the most super-duper academically organized way to go (at least according to Cindy Pang, who is only the most brilliant student at

Burroughs Junior High—and possibly the entire industrialized world—and I'll believe anything she says when it comes to scholastics . . .), but I must have been studying too late one night and been tired or something. Because right there under Monday, October 16, is a big fat goose egg of nothing where ORAL PRESENTATION should be written.

Great.

For the first time in the history of my life I was going to tank at school. I blew it. Big-time.

CHAPTER 2

At that moment I saw Ms. Pitt flash by, ridiculous peasant skirt trailing behind. She was a swirling dervish, let's be honest. And as Tatum seems to think Ms. Pitt's this Second Coming, you'd imagine she would home in on my total and complete emotional breakdown, right?

Oh no.

So much for being plugged into the "teenage experience." Ms. Pitt was clearly clueless, obsessed with her own reality and oblivious to my own. I even tried to send out an emotional SOS with my eyes, pleading with her to take notice. Nothing.

Did I mention Ms. Pitt likes to be called by her first name, Carol? Oh, I know—it's cringe-worthy, right? She contends that attempts at educational formality are ridiculous and this respectability so valued in public schools is more about vacuous tradition and not rooted in truth. I contend that she should stick to the curriculum so I have a chance of getting into a good college. Anyway, when I'm a strict stubborn traditionalist and call Ms. Pitt Ms. Pitt—which is her name, thank you very much—she gently chides me and tells me to "just call me Carol. It is my name, after all, and we're all equals in this learning environment together!"

Equals?

Please. Look, I'm in this learning environment, and I've done just fine calling teachers named Mr. Evans *Mr. Evans*, not *Bob*. And I manage to learn just fine.

I heard through the grapevine that Ms. Pitt was up to chair the entire English department. Great—that probably meant "Kumbaya" lesson plans would soon follow.

Regardless, Ms. Pitt sailed past before I could disclose my unprepared-for-the-first-time-in-my-entire-life predicament. I was about to get even more upset by her dismissal when I saw her SMASH right into Mr. Wells.

As in Principal Wells. Who sits on the school board.

Ms. Pitt's Earth-friendly, reusable coffee mug contents (my guess? An organic soy chai latte) splatted all over Mr. Wells's shirt.

"Oh no! What a klutz! Could I be more clumsy? I am so so sorry!" Ms. Pitt clucked as she attempted to pat down Mr. Wells's huge chai splotch with random loose papers, only making the situation way worse.

"Oh dear. Oh my." Mr. Wells didn't do a good job of withholding his disdain.

"I think I have some Tidy Wipes in my car," Ms. Pitt offered.

"Those are ineffective. I have Shout Wipes in my office for precisely this sort of situation. And a change of clothes."

"There you go! Well, this too shall pass, eh?"

It doesn't look like it's going to pass anytime soon, I thought with a devious teeny-tiny smile on my face. I'm sorry, but it was oddly satisfying and a welcome distraction from my own dilemma. I don't think Mr. Wells and Ms. Pitt even noticed me standing there.

Mr. Wells smiled weakly. "Aren't you slated for the English department chair interview today?"

"I am indeed. I truly believe I can bring a real originality to the school's curriculum in a way standardized testing never can."

"We shall see. And let's hope this incident is NOT an omen for how today's interview will go."

And with that, Mr. Wells moved on, a big sloppy chai mess. Ms. Pitt shook her head and continued on with her crazed trek into school.

Which allowed me to get back to my panic attack, which was verging on full tilt. I could feel the blood draining from my fingers, realizing I was woefully unprepared for my oral presentation. That's the first sign—tingly fingers (which scares me that I'll have one of those Lifetime Channel diseases later in life). My breath was shallow and I couldn't focus. I felt like I was sort of underwater, and my thoughts didn't make sense. . . . It was more like an overwhelming blob of thoughts all coalescing into one confused reality.

"Hello? Hadley? Anybody home?"

I turned, vaguely recognizing this voice. I squinted into the sun and saw a fedora-wearing figure headed my way. Oh. Soup. And Nan was right behind him.

My best friend, Soup (no one has any idea why he's called that anymore, but he's had the nickname for so long now that it has stuck, and he says anything is better than Sven, his God-given name), and with him was Nan. I'm probably a wee bit closer to Soup than to Nan, and I will admit to you and only you that it makes me feel a little bit cool and vaguely urban to have a guy best friend. Soup is the coolest despite being in the marching band, and he insists if the population would just see the obscure movie *Drumline*, his life would change forever because marching bands rule. He thinks football could not be played without the support of the marching band, which I find implausible. I contend that the high school football team is not exactly counting on the marching band's version of "On Broadway" to seal the deal. I've never offered my argument to Soup personally; it seems mean.

Nan grew up for the first ten years of her life in New York City, which is only the most excellent city on the planet along with Paris (which means I've never set foot in either place). But I've read and watched enough cable to get the gist of it—New York's the best. After all, it produced Nan, who knows so much about everything, and thankfully, she is never, ever irritating about her amazing capacity for trivia. (We'll be at Pizza Hut or something and she'll randomly announce, "Did you know that in England the Speaker of the House is not allowed to speak?" To which I'll respond, "I did not know that." Because it's always true—I didn't know that.) Nan also is one of those funky beauties, who I bet people will look up in their yearbooks ten years after graduation—you know, after they know a little bit more about life and so on—and they'll realize Nan was quite the hottie and they never even noticed.

"Okay, we've only been calling your name for the past five minutes," Nan said as they both approached.

"Huh?" I was barely monosyllabic.

"You look . . . What word am I searching for?" Soup scratched his hat.

"Vacant," Nan said.

"Yeah. Vacant. What's going on?" Soup asked.

"Well, for starters, my life is over."

"But how important is your life, anyway . . . ?" Nan smiled. I did not smile back.

"I'm serious, Nan. My new Super Student Planner Plus that Cindy Pang recommended isn't that super. I totally forgot to write down that today is my oral presentation for *To Kill a Mockingbird*," I said breathlessly. Couldn't they see this was a meltdown here?

"You forgot? Hadley Fox *forgot*?? Okay, even I remembered to prepare for my oral. How is this possible?" Soup was NOT helping.

"I have no idea how it's possible!" Oh, dear. I sounded shrill.

Nan wasn't helping when she said, "Isn't it, like, a quarter of your final grade?"

With that I had to sit down. At least Soup acknowledged my panic and sat down beside me. He also put an arm around me. (Which is probably why everyone assumes we are going out. We're always together and we're usually laughing, but we've been friends for so long that we're forever in each other's "friends" column. He's also not my type at all. Besides, I have a hard enough time thinking anyone could even find me attractive.)

14

"Don't make her feel worse, Nan! She totally has low blood sugar or something," Soup protectively semi-barked to Nan.

"My blood sugar's fine. Sometimes I say that just to make sure I get dessert: say 'low blood sugar,' and the cookies and candy appear out of nowhere. Try it some-time." I paused. "Right now, this is all about me being melodramatic." I put my hands over my eyes just to prove my point.

"Hadley. You're brilliant," Soup said in his best buck-up voice. "You know that. I know that—"

"All I know is I'm the moron who FORGOT TO WRITE DOWN THAT MY ORAL PRESENTATION IS TODAY!! God, I knew something was up this morn-ing when that comet came too close to Earth. . . ."

Soup and Nan synchronized a look of worry. They do that often with me.

"But you're the smartest of the smart, Hadley. You'll be fine," Nan insisted. But I don't think she gets that to be valedictorian you cannot be fine, you have to be stel-lar. Perfect. Everything I am NOT today . . .

"Yeah, can't you just make something up?" Soup said this as if it was the easiest thing in the world.

"That's right," I said, hearing my voice take on a real smarminess. "I should just waltz into Ms. Pitt's class and start speaking in perfect paragraphs about racial injustice and how it relates to *To Kill a Mockingbird*." I knew I sounded panicked but I couldn't help myself. "Weren't we just having a really long, detailed conversation about this very topic just the other day, Soup? Oh yeah . . . I really feel an A-plus coming on!"

"You always get so weird when things don't go exactly your way," Soup said with as much anger as I've ever heard come out of him. "All I was doing was trying to help!"

Soup and Nan shared a quick look (yet again) and bolted, leaving me sitting there in my panicky, apparently weirdo state. Watching them march off, I instantly felt terrible. "I'm sorry! It's just who I am!"

Soup turned on his heels and stared me down. "I know! That's the problem!"

Ouch.

Double ouch.

Why did I have to be me sometimes?

CHAPTER 3

On my way into school, I saw Milly Albright approaching, mostly because it's impossible to miss those braces glimmering under the fluorescent lighting. Milly's smile was massive, but it wasn't entirely convincing. I always sensed a sadness lurking nearby despite her huge grin.

"HEY, HADLEY!" Milly singsonged.

"Hey, Milly," I said, and wanted to keep in motion.

"You okay?! You seem sorta down!" Milly asked with way too much enthusiasm. Poor thing. She really was sincere (which, truth be told, only made the situation worse).

"I'll be fine," I mumbled.

"Maybe you should stop by the You Rock! Self Matters! group after school. Because it really does rock!"

Oh, boy.

A school group on self-esteem was *so* not in the cards today. (Or ever, for that matter.) Besides, I'd seen the motley collection of students who attended Ms. Pitt's weird group with tragically low enrollment. That self-esteem group could use some self-esteem.

"I'm sorta tied up today, Milly," I said, and saw her eyes cloud with rejection. "But thanks for the offer."

"You betcha then! See ya!" Milly turned and headed off, bobbing like a human pogo stick. Milly gave off the distinct aura that she would always be unable to find the rhythm for the clap-along at the end of any concert.

As I watched Milly awkwardly navigate down the hallway, I realized that thus far, junior high had been a colossal disappointment.

I had always imagined junior high would mean having boyfriends and getting big groups to go to the water park together on hot summer days. But there's no boyfriend in sight and the closest water park is in San Diego, and since no one drives yet, the water park is out.

So for now, junior high is about groups on self-esteem and the like.

I had hoped things at junior high would be more adult, more civil. . . . Wrong. It's just more homework. Sometimes I miss the elementary school slumber parties and pizza parties and getting way too excited about owning a hamster (which for all intents and purposes is a worthless pet). It was also a whole lot easier to get gold stars and

TERRIFIC! written across the top of papers.

Maybe I thought things would be great at junior high because things looked great for Tatum. She always had this cool posse of friends coming and going when she was in junior high, and they did exciting things together, like going to the beach. Her hair was always in place and she styled it several different ways, all of which were flattering and fabulous. She IM'd at night with her friends, which in my estimation was ridiculously glamorous. What secrets were they sharing? Glossy, gossipy, important ones, I was convinced. Tatum went to dances, wore kitten heels, and wore lotions that smelled like yummy fruit.

Anyway, maybe it wasn't as great for Tatum as it seemed to me, but I was really bummed to realize, when I finally got to junior high, I didn't evolve into her. I stayed the same wound-too-tight Hadley. What a letdown.

And Lord, how I wish I could be Tatum Fox when I walked down the hall. Heads would turn and things would happen. I just know with every fiber in my being that Zane Henderson would absolutely, most definitely, positively notice me if that were the case.

Okay. Let me back up. Zane Henderson, second only to Ryan Gosling in *The Notebook*, is the love of my life. For one, Zane has green eyes. Not brown eyes with flecks of green, but green eyes. Like piercing Hulk green, almost otherworldly. Nan disagrees and says they're really more hazel but she's wrong. For another thing, he wore an old Police T-shirt once (not the-long-arm-of-the-law police, but the band the Police) to school. While most stuff from the eighties sounds, well, like cheeseball stuff from the eighties, the Police's music STILL rocks. I thought that was really cool and I just know we could have long conversations about how awesome their lyrics are . . . because I'm sure Zane is the sort of guy who actually pays attention to the lyrics themselves. (Take "Everything Little Thing She Does Is Magic" and the genius lyric: "It's a big enough umbrella, but it's always me that ends up getting wet." That pretty much sums up my life so far.)

Bottom line, Zane isn't a muscle-head moron. At least I sure hope not . . . I don't know him particularly well. Let's just say we haven't exactly had a lot of conversations. There was a "hey" back in September (which was staggeringly fabulous) and nothing since. But in my fantasy-prone mind, Zane and I just talk and talk and go to the beach and he always remembers my favorite sandwich is egg salad, which is really an underrated sandwich. Zane's so thoughtful that way.

And since I'm in flat-out fantasy mode here . . . let me just come right out and say it. Okay. So how cool does Hadley Henderson sound? Doesn't it have great alliteration and sound wonderful together? I know it's antifeminist, blah blah blah, but still, it does, right? And hey, my grandparents met when they were eleven. Stranger things have happened. . . .

Soup thinks Zane's a quasi-dork and pointed out he's never heard him say much. I contend Zane's just misunderstood and shy. That can happen to boys, too, I suppose.

Of course it makes perfect sense that Zane Henderson should choose this Monday to actually speak to me. The Monday on which my friends are angry at me and my skin has a sick whitish pallor. The day my eyes are crazed and panicked. If Zane were to speak to me, I would hope it would be a Friday when there was a buzz of anticipation in the air and at least my hair would look semi-decent. But oh no. He had to speak to me today.

I had grabbed my books out of my locker. (And for the record, I do not decorate my locker. I get so tired of everyone trying to show how cool they are by their locker decor. It's like: *Look at all the concerts I've been to! See the concert stubs? Don't I have great taste when it comes to music?! And see these pictures I have up—don't I just have the most friends ever?!* Anyway, in protest, I refuse to hang one darn thing and all you can see in my locker is foul brown paint and books.)

I was making my way to first-period English, my head ponging with thoughts of panic about my oral presentation and whether my friends would forgive my weirdness. That's when I saw Zane. He was leaning against his locker and I was positive he sort of lit up when he saw me. At least I think that's what happened. Maybe there was someone behind me? I turned to see who he was looking at, but apparently he seemed to recognize me. Me being the one with the wild eyes and clammy white skin, remember.

"Uh, hey. Hadley," Zane offered as I approached in virtual slow-motion.

Was this happening? Was Zane speaking to ME?

"Uh, yeah," I responded. I mentioned I was witty, right? I was extremely proud of that especially frothy response. *Uh, yeah?*

"Hey," he responded back.

Hadn't he already said "hey"? Who cares, it was something. "Hey," I volleyed yet again. Keep it going. . . .

"So, uh, I was wondering if I, uh, saw you this weekend."

What? You were wondering if you saw ME this weekend? "Oh yeah?" I said in a very squeaky dork voice. My body was leaving me, floating above the halls of Burroughs Junior High, observing me being a monosyllabic moron.

"Yeah." He grinned and I grinned back. God, this was surreal! We were grinning at each other—I'm absolutely certain of it! And of course my hand reached for my hair and I did one of those lame-o hand-comb moves I had seen all the cheerleaders do before—you know, where they flick their hair ever-so-shampoo-commercially. I always thought it looked so fakey-flirty—the hand through the hair, that is—but I didn't realize until that very moment that the gesture truly is grounded in instinct. You like a boy, he's talking to you, and whammo! You just have to use your fingers to do a comb-through of the hair! I had no idea! It was like I was an ACTUAL TEENAGER!

"Because, uh, I was at a tennis match," Zane said, continuing with his fantastic conversation that absolutely had me floating.

"Oh yeah?"

"And I was wondering . . . isn't your sister on the tennis team?"

WHAT?

Zane must have seen my total teenager smile melt off my face. Actually, it felt like I was losing more than just a smile, it also felt like there was actual flesh dripping off. You know, like at the end of *Raiders of the Lost Ark*.

"Tatum? Isn't she your sister?"

Of course. He loves Tatum. Everyone loves Tatum.

God, for a nanosecond I actually entertained the idea that it was possible for someone—preferably a boy and more preferably, Zane Henderson—to actually find me attractive. How stupid could I be? "Uh, yeah. She is."

"She's good." He smiled to himself, probably lost in the thought of Tatum's teen-dream face.

Oh, did I mention to you that Tatum's on the high school tennis team and undefeated this year as the number one singles player? I know. It gets worse, right?

"At tennis, I mean, she's good. Because I saw her play. You know, at the high school. Against Thompson Valley, I think." Was his face getting red?

"She's undefeated." I tried to smile but it felt like my face was betraying me. I might pass out. . . .

"Cool. Anyway . . . thought maybe you were there, so . . ."

"Nope, I didn't see her match. I had a lot of homework this weekend. I had to make a model of an atom for science. I almost chose a walnut shell." And the walnut shell nugget helped me look that much more cool! I should spare him this torture and end this exchange now. He didn't want to speak to me, anyway. He just wanted the Tatum 4-1-1. "So I'll see ya," I managed to squeak out.

"Yeah. I've got my oral presentation. . . ." And with

that, Zane strolled into Ms. Pitt's English class and panic reflooded my body. Great. Not only was the love of my life salivating over my sister, but I was about to have my first and most thunderous academic failure.

CHAPTER 4

I walked into class with what must have been a pretty stunned expression on my face. Nan swooped up and whispered, "I forgive you for being a freak, if and only if you tell me that Zane Henderson just asked you out."

"Nan. This is me you're dealing with, remember? Of course he didn't ask me out." Again, I couldn't feel my fingers, I swear.

"Why not? Boys—and this does not apply to our Soup—don't talk to girls otherwise. I mean, what would we ever talk about with them about? Football?"

"No. Tennis, apparently."

"He likes you. I could tell—"

Before Nan could say another word, I cut her off and whispered, "Zane likes Tatum. That's all he wanted to talk about."

"Oh."

I concurred. "I know. Of course, right?"

Nan tried to make me feel better, I'll give her that. "Maybe he just—"

"He went to see Tatum play at the tennis match this weekend. He said she's so talented or something."

"Oh." This "oh" sounded more defeated. Nan gave me a "buck up" half grin. "Man, your day REALLY isn't going well, is it."

"Thanks for reminding me," I responded.

Just then, there was a—

GONG!

Ms. Pitt's gong started class. She always struck that annoying gong and did a little Chinese bow to the class. It was just so organic-fruit of her and wannabe-hippie obvious—you know, like slapping a LOVE ANIMALS, DON'T EAT THEM! bumper sticker on your Prius or something. Come to think of it, I think Ms. Pitt may have that exact bumper sticker on that exact car. . . .

And now it was too late to approach her and plead my case. . . . I needed an extension, a get-out-of-jail-free card, something. I had to try. "Ms. Pitt, could I speak to you?" I asked. "It's really—"

"After class, Hadley. Okay? We have a big day—I think you're making your oral presentation today, aren't you?" Ms. Pitt surveyed the room, barely scanning my obviously desperate face. Nothing was registering with Ms. Pitt.

"That's what I wanted to talk to you about—"

"You're not sick?"

"Well, no—"

"No family tragedy or anything?"

"No." She was so impossible!

"Then it can wait until after class when I am more than available." She smiled at me and gestured for me to take my seat.

How could anyone be more clueless??

I walked back to my seat like I was being led to my lethal injection. Soup, who sits in front of me, saw my state and said, "Dead man walking!" Soup thought this was hilarious.

"Not funny." I put my head down on my desk.

"I shouldn't be talking to you, anyway. You have GOT to learn how to chill—"

Ms. Pitt gestured "shhh" to Soup, and the school announcements began over the PA. She pointed to the speaker on the wall, indicating its grave importance. I failed to see why information about book drives and cafeteria lunch specials were that essential.

"Good morning, fellow Mustangs, this is your Student Council President, Kaya Tisch, with some biiiiig news!" Kaya Tisch was so over the top, she even made sunny Milly Albright seem like Buzzkill Betty.

Let me tell ya, Kaya Tisch was not even vaguely disappointed with the junior high experience. Not in the slightest. She was vibrating with glee and joy and profound enthusiasm. She was a walking rainbow.

"Tonight is a Burroughs Junior High first, and I am SO psyched to tell you about it now! And believe me, there was some SERIOUS arm-twisting behind the scenes to get this to happen, but when I ran for Student Council President I promised I would deliver FUN, NEW activities for the school, and Kaya Tisch is DELIVERING on her campaign promise!"

I couldn't take it. Maybe I was already dead and this was officially hell.

"So! Let me get RIGHT to it!"

"We're waiting. . . ." Soup said, and I had to nearly smile. Nearly.

"Surprise! Tonight is the inaugural I-Hate-Mondays DANCE! It's the first dance EVER in the history of the school on a MONDAY!" Kaya might explode from glee. *"Because if you hate Mondays like I hate Mondays, then we ALL deserve a big change of pace! It is going to be SO cool!"*

Maybe Zane can ask Tatum to chaperone, I thought bitterly to myself as I stared over at his sublime profile. God, the way he was studying a pencil was beautiful.

"Oh, joy. I've *always* wanted to celebrate *Monday*," Nan noted darkly. Despite Nan's snarky comment, the class seemed to buzz with a low-grade excitement. I had to hand it to Kaya—an impromptu Monday-night dance was different. And . . . what if Zane wanted to talk about Tatum more at the dance? At least we'd be talking, right?

"So we'll see you all there in the school cafeteria, eight P.M. TONIGHT!" You'd think Kaya had single-handedly coordinated Middle East peace.

Ms. Pitt stepped forward to quell the hubbub. "All right, class, all right. Let's all settle down, we've got a lot to tackle this morning."

Right, like my total downfall.

"We've got to get right to our *To Kill a Mocking-bird* oral presentations if we're to get through them all. I so look forward to your thoughts and what you have to share with the class," said Ms. Pitt. "To start the day, I'd also like to share a review I found this weekend from *The Washington Post*, which originally ran about this transcendent book." Ms. Pitt paused for dramatic effect. *"'A hundred pounds of sermons of tolerance will weigh far less in the scale of enlightenment than a mere 18 ounces of new fiction bearing the title* To Kill a Mockingbird.'" Ms. Pitt paused and placed a hand on her heart, suggesting to what degree she was moved. (Which was big-time, apparently.)

Her emotional moment was interrupted by a knock at the door. She went to answer it and the A/V librarian technician with astoundingly poor posture rolled in a TV and DVD. "Delivery for Henderson?"

Zane raised his hand, and Ms. Pitt was clearly thrown. Zane said, "That's for me. It's for my oral presentation." Ms. Pitt's face registered concern.

"You didn't discuss using visual aids. . . ."

Zane pulled a DVD out of his bag. "I thought you'd be okay with it. My mom says it's a classic. Is that cool?"

"Well, what is it?" Ms. Pitt was more exasperated than usual. That made two of us.

"*In Cold Blood*. And don't worry, Ms. Pitt. Because in this scene no one dies or swears or is naked or anything." The class twittered at that one.

Ms. Pitt sat down at her desk and gestured to go on. I wouldn't have allowed A/V equipment in *my* classroom, even if it had been requested by Zane Henderson.

"Okay. So," Zane started with his trademark understated grace. "This movie's about this sick murder that really took place in Kansas in nineteen fifty-nine. Here, let me show ya."

Zane hit PLAY and a grim scene played out in which

two guys shot an entire family. It was horrible even though you didn't see *that* much actual gore. My mind was reeling:

1. My oral presentation is going to *tank*. Crash and burn. Fiery death. Plagues and locusts and famine.

2. What in the world does this violent scene have to do with *To Kill a Mockingbird* again?

3. Why is Ms. Pitt so oblivious to positively everything exactly?

But more important:

4. Then again, who cared? This oral presentation gave me an excuse to stare at Zane Henderson without any risk of looking like a stalker. At least I had that going for me.

Zane hit STOP and pivoted toward the class. His face got a bit red and you could tell he was shy. It was painfully endearing, like he was my own little secret. "So, uh . . . you're probably wondering what, uh, this movie has to do with *To Kill a Mockingbird*."

Sally Kirk raised her hand. "I know! I know!"

Zane paused, unsure how to respond.

"Both movies are in black-and-white?" She waited expectantly with moon eyes.

"Uh, what?" responded Zane. In his defense, her answer was lame.

"*To Kill a Mockingbird*? We watched it in class? And it was in black-and-white, too?" Sally spoke in perpetual question marks.

"Oh, yeah. But no. See, this movie is based on the book *In Cold Blood*, which is by Truman Capote. That famous author, I think he's dead, and he was like four feet tall."

Blank stares. Maybe my presentation couldn't be too much worse than this. . . .

"Anyway, *In Cold Blood* was written by Truman Capote and he was the best friend of Harper Lee, who wrote *To Kill a Mockingbird*. They grew up in the South together and supposedly the character of Dill is based on Truman."

He pulled out a picture of Truman Capote and displayed it for the class. Unfortunately, the picture was practically postage-stamp minuscule and even when straining, you could barely see him. Teddy Hasert (who had the largest head on the planet, though it contained a rather tiny brain), sat in the front row, and apparently he could see the picture: "Oh yeah. I know that dude."

"Harper Lee went to Kansas with Truman to do research for the book and stayed there for, like, years. Or a really long time at least, you know, interviewing people and stuff. They say he couldn't have written it without her." Zane paused, and Ms. Pitt finally jumped in.

"How many people knew this before Zane's presentation, the connection between Harper Lee and Truman Capote?"

One hand went up. Sally Kirk. Of course. Actually I knew, too, but I didn't want to be in the Sally Kirk smarty-pants world.

Ms. Pitt smiled at Sally. "So most of us have learned something today. Zane, why is the book *In Cold Blood* so important?"

Crickets were chirping somewhere. "Uh . . . because . . ."

Ms. Pitt tried to help him along. "Because it was a revolutionary event of literature—"

"—that blurred the line between, you know . . . reality and fiction," Zane blurted, almost stunning himself. "When Truman Capote wrote it, he used, like, newspaper writing and then he combined it with creative writing, basically."

34

Ms. Pitt raised her eyebrows. "Very good. And how did his writing change because of Harper Lee?"

"Well, we'll never know. I wasn't there. Just as Capote wasn't there the night Perry and Smith killed that family in Holcomb, Kansas." He sort of smiled, maybe a bit proud. That was it. I was officially in love. I knew he was the sort who had to be coaxed and once they were on a roll, they'd be unstoppable. "But I can imagine that Truman as a . . . well, let's just say not a lot of dudes like Truman were showing up much in Kansas. He was pretty flamboyant and I bet having Harper with him made the townspeople open up and trust him more. I bet he got a better story because of her."

"And I bet you're right. Great work, Zane. Okay, Hadley. You're up next."

Soup and Nan spun in their seats and shot daggers my way. I froze in my chair.

"Hadley? I said you're up." I had no choice. I felt myself walk to the front of the classroom, empty-handed. No oral presentation to cling to and read from. My heart thump-thumped, thump-thumped in my chest.

"Whenever you're ready . . ." Ms. Pitt offered.

Except I wasn't ready. I was dying! Couldn't she see that?

35

Ms. Pitt cleared her throat as if to say "begin already."

I cleared my throat in response. And gulped. I had to begin. "So, uh . . . *To Kill a Mockingbird*. Great book. Harper Lee knows how to write a book. And she did write one. Which is the one we read." I just knew it, I couldn't put any thoughts together. My head was swirling.

Nan and Soup shared a look and I knew this was going to be as bad as I thought. Ms. Pitt leaned in, concerned.

"So the book . . . the book was," I heard myself say. Was that even a sentence? "*To Kill a Mockingbird*. I mentioned that . . . is about this girl. I mean it is and it isn't. There's also a trial, so . . ." The room was getting fuzzy.

"Hadley, isn't your topic about how race impacts justice?" Ms. Pitt said.

I just nodded vaguely.

"Would you like to talk about that, then?"

Zane was wincing while he watched me, as if he was sucking on lemons. *Focus, focus, focus, you idiot! Think of something!*

"Um . . . yeah. So O. J. Simpson . . . ?"

"What about him?"

"He, uh . . . well, you know . . . I have no idea," I mumbled. This was more pronounced than any other panic attack I'd ever had. I was defenseless and mute.

"Hadley, I need to speak to you in the hallway." Ms. Pitt trotted out of the class into the hall and I had no choice but to follow.

I had never hated a Monday more in my entire life.

CHAPTER 5

"Hadley. This is so unlike you," Ms. Pitt stated the obvious.

All I could do was look down, humiliated. I had never ever in my life been called into the hall by a teacher.

"I know it's unlike me. I tried to tell you before!" was my only defense.

"Okay, so tell me now. I'm listening." Ms. Pitt gave me her best "I-really-get-you" eyes. Which only made me know how much she *didn't* get me.

"I switched to this Super Student Planner Plus organizer thing and I guess I spaced on writing down the date. I'm so, so sorry, but I forgot."

Ms. Pitt's eyes grew like saucers. "*You* forgot?"

All I could do was nod yes. "Maybe I could have an extension? I'll skip the dance and cram tonight and—"

"I'm sorry, Hadley, but absolutely not. Forgetting is not a justifiable reason, I'm afraid. If I gave a free pass to everyone who forgot, where would we be?" Ms. Pitt gave a tough-love smile as my head figuratively exploded.

Come on, haven't I proven worthy of just one little tiny exception? My mind scrambled—without my oral presentation, an A in English would be virtually impossible. This was the beginning of the end. I wouldn't get into Stanford. I wouldn't even get into Chico State. I'd end up folding sweaters at the Gap or . . . worse!—panhandling in the streets of LA or . . .

Ms. Pitt's voice interrupted my increasingly paranoid thoughts. "I remember once when Tatum came in unprepared—"

When I heard *Tatum*, a fuse blew in my head. The rip cord was pulled and this crazy monster of emotions opened up its mouth and swallowed me whole.

"AGAIN WITH TATUM! Why is everyone talking about Tatum? She's awesome, I get it!" I couldn't believe how loud that came out, but it was almost like an out-of-body experience. I had no control.

Ms. Pitt stepped back, shocked apparently by my outburst. But there was no stopping me now. . . . Everything was boiling over and I kept going. "I can't believe you chair up the committee on self-esteem! Rule number one—don't compare the geeky sister to her gorgeous older sister! EVER!"

Ms. Pitt's eyes were filled with instant recognition. "Hadley, you are far from geeky. But I realize how someone's self-image can be completely divorced from all reality whatsoever. You feel inadequate. I understand. And I know that must be hard for you. It's clear your sense of self is contorted, much like a psychological fun-house mirror in which—"

"*'Psychological fun-house mirror'? What?*" I had to catch my breath.

"I am merely trying to understand how you feel here!"

"Then maybe you should stop trying!"

Ms. Pitt was exasperated. "Can we continue this discussion after school and come up with an adequate solution?"

I nodded hotly yes.

"And I vow to never mention Tatum again, as I realize having a sister so dynamic must be—"

I stormed away, before I did Ms. Pitt bodily harm. If it wasn't completely clear, I didn't want to talk about Tatum's "dynamism," either. Ms. Pitt was so dense! And she was the worst kind of dense—the sort of dense who *thinks* they've got it all figured out and are totally plugged in, but it turns out they're as clueless as the day is long.

Before I entered class, I felt Ms. Pitt touch my shoulder. I spun around and glared. I have never lost my cool so much in front of a teacher in my life. "What?"

"I assume you've read the book."

"Of course," I said, adding defensively: "I wrote down all the vocab words I didn't know and everything!"

Ms. Pitt shook her head, disappointed. "Oh, Hadley. *To Kill a Mockingbird* is not about vocab words. . . . It's about life. . . ." She looked me in the eyes. "Do you know what it's about? I mean, really about?"

I was tired of being so defensive and was already emotionally raw. "Look, I read it, okay?! I did the assignment!"

Ms. Pitt cut me off, frayed herself. "So you said, so you said." She took a big breath. "How about you give a more general presentation on the book itself and we'll reassess after we've *both* cooled down."

"Fine." Things can't stink any more, so why not? My life was over, anyway. Any drop of prior confidence I ever possessed leaked out of my body. I was a shell.

I stood in front of the class and looked out, the whole class staring with disbelief. Nan and Soup were shell-shocked, and worse, Zane could barely make eye contact.

Ms. Pitt handed me her copy of *To Kill a Mockingbird*.

I flipped open the book and it almost magically—and I don't use terms like "magically" unless I mean it—stopped on page 138. At least it seriously felt like the book willed itself to stop in a certain spot. My eyes found a passage that seemed to leap off the page. You know in movies when the camera wants to direct your attention to something in particular, so there's almost like a little spotlight on the item in question? Well, it was sort of like that. Not that I saw an actual light from Moses on the hill or anything, it was more like it was a . . . feeling. Or something.

"This quote is from Atticus, the father." I cleared my throat. "'*You,* uh, *never really understand a person until you consider things from his point of view—*'" Deep breath.

"I wanna understand your *sister's* point of view!" some meathead moron blurted from the back of the room. "Tatum Fox is HOT!"

Someone howled.

With that, I dropped my book. It was all too much. Why oh why couldn't a hole appear in the floor and I could just dive right in and disappear forever?

I tried to finish the quote and look strong. "'Until you . . . until . . .'"

Ms. Pitt did try to come to my aid and help me along. She bent down, picked up my dropped book, and said,

" '—until you climb into—' "

And together, Ms. Pitt and I finished the quote aloud: " '. . . *his skin and walk around in it.*' "

What happened next sounds made up but I swear it is completely true.

The clock minute hand snapped back one minute.

The lights flickered.

I felt a jolt.

It seemed as if the world had been tipped off its axis and was settling back into its usual holding pattern.

Ms. Pitt and I just stood there, uncertain what had just happened. And what *had* happened again exactly?

"No way! Did the clock totally just snap back and the lights go postal or am I completely hallucinating here?" I exclaimed.

And then everything gets even weirder. Because while I, Hadley Fox, had asked that question, what I heard was Ms. Pitt's voice!

When I turned around, trying to gain just a smidge of clarity or sanity or anything to cling to, I realized I was standing next to—get this—*me*! NEXT TO HADLEY! Panicked, I looked down at myself, and that was a shock, let me tell you. Because I would NEVER, *EVER* dress like a wannabe earth mother, but it seemed I was wearing a flowy peasant skirt. I would never own a flowy peasant skirt, let alone wear one to school!

Then I studied my hands . . . and they were *so* not my hands, they were ancient and covered with bizarre rings! Those dorky rings that are only sold in artisan shops where they sell a lot of ceramic bowls and wind chimes. There's also almost always a cat named Sage or something ambling around the store.

Anyway, they were Ms. Pitt's hands! WHAT??

Wait a second! I APPEARED TO BE—AND YOU KNOW I COULDN'T MAKE THIS UP IF I TRIED—MS. PITT! You probably think I'm crazy right about now, but don't worry, I was thinking the same thing.

"Maybe it was some sort of seismic shift. . . . I felt it, too," I watched HADLEY say. Except *I* hadn't said anything!

But there "Hadley" was, wearing the same cargo pants and marginally cool T-shirt and striped hoodie I had put on this morning! Standing right there in class! It was me, but it wasn't me. Was this some sort of molecular mix-up? Some glitch in the physics of the universe? What was happening?

We turned to stare at each other, totally weirded out.

"What's going on?!" I whispered, panicky. Again, that was definitely Ms. Pitt's voice coming out of my mouth, not mine.

Let me say right here that from now on I'll have to call Ms.-Pitt-inhabiting-my-body "Hadley." And I'll have to call myself "Ms. Pitt." (Ugh!)

"Class, did anyone feel anything?" Hadley asked. "Zane?"

The class was silent, freaked, sharing stolen looks of complete worry. I know what they were thinking: Why was Hadley addressing the class this way?

"Uh, no . . . I didn't feel anything. . . ." Zane responded uneasily.

"Dude! This is so freakin' weird!" another meathead (there are a lot of them at Burroughs Junior High) astutely observed from the back row.

Both of our pairs of eyes were scared and wide, scanning each other and the room. "Hallway. Now," Hadley said, and dragged me into the hallway. Or rather, the "me" in question was Ms. Pitt. Hadley closed the door to the classroom to give us some privacy in the hallway.

"What are you doing?" I asked.

"No, what are YOU doing?" Hadley responded.

"There is no possible way you could . . . be me . . . is there?" I squawked. "NO!!! No, no, no! This is not possible!" I practically screamed, and pulled at Ms. Pitt's way-too-much hair.

"I mean, did we fall into a portal or something? Because I *so* do not need my life to go all *Matrix* on me!" Except it wasn't me at all. Again, my voice sounded entirely too much like Ms. Pitt. To make matters worse, Mr. Wells appeared out of nowhere and stared at us incredulously.

"Ah, Mr. Wells. Hello there," Hadley said officiously with the distinct sound of near-panic creeping into her voice. "We were discussing . . . movie imagery."

"Movie imagery?" He didn't buy it.

"Right. From the movie *The Matrix*." Oh, boy.

"I see," he said skeptically. "And where are your students, Ms. Pitt?"

"They're in there," I said, gesturing to the classroom. Couldn't he just get lost already?

"*In there*, how comforting . . ." With that, Mr. Wells walked on but the disdain was heavy. He looked back suspiciously over his shoulder a few times.

"*In there?* Okay, there is NO way you are going to MY English department chair interview today. Not talking like that, you're not!" Hadley said.

"Back up. English chair interviews are *so* not important right now," I tried to say calmly. Focus, focus. . . . "Okay, it was the *To Kill a Mockingbird* quote that did this. We said the quote together and that's when this . . . this . . . impossible weirdness happened, right?"

Hadley nodded yes.

"Then let's say it again. Maybe we'll switch back!" I cleared my throat, a little proud of myself—that would do it, very clever solution. See, I *am* an honor student, after all. . . . "*'You never really understand a person until you consider things from his point of view—'*"

I gave Hadley a look and she joined in: "*'—and climb into his skin and walk around in it.'*"

We both stared at each other, expecting another lights-flicker, body-switching moment.

Nothing.

Crap.

I closed my eyes tightly, scrambling for an answer when I heard an—

"Ohmmm . . . ohmmm . . ." Hadley also had her eyes closed, and her thumb and middle finger were touching as if in some prayer mode.

"What are you doing?"

"Releasing my need to the universe," Hadley said with pseudo-calm.

"I don't release my need to the universe!"

"You should," Hadley said as if this was totally logical. "Obviously the universe is trying to tell us something."

"Yeah, that we're INSANE." I paused for effect and

finally Hadley opened her eyes.

"All right. We'll deal with the interview later . . . right now we have to get back into class before we both get thrown out of school *permanently*," Hadley said, and started to march back into class, just as uppity as Ms. Pitt would have done.

Wait a second! I thought. *If this is really happening, why not use this hallucination? I'm suddenly the teacher, right? The one with the power for once?! So, why not give me and Zane a reason to interact? Brilliant! I may wake up any moment, but let's use this—*

We entered the classroom and everyone looked at us like we had fourteen heads. Soup and Nan gave a freaked "what gives?" shrug of the shoulders, searching our faces for clues.

Out of instinct, Ms. Pitt—I mean, Hadley—stepped forward to handle the class. "So, class—"

But that looked even more insane. Hadley can't run this classroom! I stepped in front of her. After all, I was in Ms. Pitt's body, right?

I stopped for a moment, to think about how Ms. Pitt would have run the class. And I almost—truly—did her a favor and considered behaving like her. But then I thought: *You're* in charge. Why don't you run things the way *you* want? After all, *Hadley's* not going to get into trouble for anything Ms. Pitt does wrong.

"Okay, there's going to be a little change-up here," I said.

"There is?" asked Hadley, clearly threatened.

"Yup! I'm going to team up students. Let's start up . . . Zane and Hadley. How about that?" I smiled, gesturing for Hadley to sit down already.

"Why?" Hadley asked.

"Because I'm the teacher and I said so." I smiled to myself. That *was* fun to say. Power *does* corrupt!

"We have definitely entered an unsafe zone," observed Nan.

Just then, there was a knock at the door and Kaya Tisch appeared dressed as a giant heart. Yup . . . exactly what we needed right about now.

"It's Student Council's Candy-Grams delivery time!" Kaya chirped.

"Candy-Grams are beyond pointless," I muttered. That's why I hadn't bought any last week when they were selling them. Plus, I knew I wouldn't get one from anybody, so why bother. Hadley lightly punched me in the arm in protest, and Kaya turned in mock horror, reacting as if I had just run over a box of puppies. I guess it was sorta strange for Ms. Pitt to object to Candy-Grams. She lives for these "student-directed interchanges."

"Why would you say that, Ms. Pitt? You *chair* Student Council, remember?!" Kaya asked incredulously.

Oh. Right. "Yeah. That's cool," I offered weakly, which clearly did little to convince anyone of Ms. Pitt's sanity. "Let's just get this over with, then."

Kaya gulped and tried to put on her best happy-time face. She pulled out construction-paper hearts from a bag.

"So these Candy-Grams are the kickoff for our I Hate Mondays Dance, which will be totally awesome!" I gestured a mini "woo-hoo" and twirled my fingers.

Of course Hadley wasn't having any of that and swiped my hand down.

"Pat Offenbacher!" Kaya delivered Pat a Candy-Gram heart and he treated it with complete indifference.

"Renee Loomis!" Renee seemed way more excited about her heart.

"Ms. Pitt!"

With the announcement of Ms. Pitt getting a Candy-Gram, the whole class burst into a suggestive *WOOOO!*

I turned to Hadley. "Okay, who sent YOU a Candy-Gram?"

Hadley's eyes said it all. "Uh, don't you mean YOUR Candy-Gram, Ms. Pitt?"

"Oh. Right. My Candy-Gram! Let me see that!" I

snagged the Candy-Gram and dug into it. I read aloud, "'Be Mine! XO, Mr. H.'" I thought about it for a beat. "No way, Mr. Hudson?! Nice, he's quasi-adorable!"

Hadley covered her mouth with her hand, clearly pondering this delivery.

"Okay, cue the theme to *Twilight Zone*," Soup joked. The class burst into uncomfortable laughter.

Just then Kaya came back into the classroom. "Sorry, I almost forgot one. It's for Hadley Fox from a Secret Admirer."

I jumped into the air. I GOT A CANDY-GRAM?

Except the class—whose collective heads were going to explode from confusion anyway—wasn't exactly expecting Ms. Pitt to leap for joy. I looked at Soup and Nan with a big dorky smile and they just cringed back.

But seriously, who could this be from? I was also for the record a bit horrified that despite the fact I seemed to have, oh, you know, SWITCHED BODIES WITH MY TEACHER, I was still capable of obsessing about a secret admirer Candy-Gram.

Mr. Wells peered into the classroom, double-checking to see if the prior weirdness was continuing. And was it ever.

Instinctively, Ms. Pitt waved—and never before had Mr. Wells seen Hadley Fox so excited to see him. She flopped her hand around until she realized Hadley probably wouldn't respond that way, and then she awkwardly put her hand down. This only confirmed his internal *Hmmm*, I'm sure.

"So, Zane. I guess you better get into your newly formed group, huh?" I said. As Hadley begrudgingly walked toward him, I whispered, "Be cool."

I leaned over to Zane and kindly offered, "And if you ever need an English tutor or anything like that, Zane, I am SO at your service. . . ."

"Gross," Soup whispered to himself.

I was smiling at Zane in a vaguely flirty, liberated way and realized it may have seemed just a wee bit predatory. Major creepy chills. So I dialed back the smile and moved on.

Zane's friend Blake witnessed this and leaned over. "Dude, Ms. Pitt is fine. She can totally tutor me anytime she wants. . . ." Zane's only response was a weirded-out look.

Unbelievably, the school bell rang. Apparently body-switching is a time-consuming business and the whole forty-eight minutes had passed. Everyone got up in a daze to exit class. Hadley (and it is SO strange to stare at yourself, like it's a mirror, but there's no mirror there!) and I shared a look and realized she should leave the class and follow the students. After all, Hadley's a student, right?

I leaned over and whispered to Hadley, "Locker combination is twenty-four, fourteen, twenty-four. Easy. And second period I have home ec with Mrs. Bird. We're making strudel. Don't ask."

Before she could respond, Zane approached. As in approached me when I wasn't even me! Perfect!

"So, Hadley . . ."

I stood back and willed Ms. Pitt NOT to make me look, sound, or act like a freak. "Yes, Zane?" Oh, jeez, that sounded like I was forty-two years old! And even Ms. Pitt wasn't forty-two! It seemed that once she was in my body, Ms. Pitt decided to get in touch with her most matronly, stuffy-shirt self.

"So you, uh, going to the dance tonight?" Zane stammered.

Every hair on my body stood on end. Was I hearing this??

"Yes, I suppose I should," Hadley said.

"Cool. See you there, then," Zane offered, and darted off.

I swooped up to Hadley and repeated what I had just heard. "'See you there, then'?" I whispered excitedly.

Hadley clearly was not grasping the all-consuming amazingness of this. "Yes, I've always suspected Zane was interested in you."

"*Shut! Up!*" I squealed, and again, more students turned to stare. I guess teachers don't routinely talk like they're cast members on *The Real World*.

"He pretends to look at the posters on the wall, but I suspect he's looking at you."

"No way! There is no possible way Zane Enter-Middle-Name-Here Henderson could possibly like me!" My wheels were spinning now. "I mean, he's probably in love with Tatum and only wants to get near her. Right?"

"We really have bigger—"

"BUT . . . even if he IS interested, which I'm suggesting he is because, after all, I am me, right? BUT even if he IS interested, of course this would have to happen on the day I'm in my TEACHER'S BODY!"

I glanced up and saw Nan and Soup approaching. I walked away, but only far enough to make it *look* like I couldn't hear.

"Okay, what is going on?" they asked the Hadley substitute.

"On? Nothing," Hadley responded. Good so far.

"Yeah, what was that with Ms. Pitt? I know you've always thought she was lame, but—"

"Wait, *lame? I think Ms. Pitt is lame?*" Hadley's voice

was so hurt. Ooops. Ms. Pitt was going to be in for some surprises today.

"Duh. She's always going on about Tatum and you hate that. You are seriously wacked this morning. Did someone spike your OJ this morning or something?"

"No, I don't drink! Ever! Do I?"

"Caffeine's as dark as you get. Wait. Why am I telling *you* what *you* do again?" Nan turned to Soup. "Does this make any sense to you?"

"None," Soup said, and took off.

As I eavesdropped on this exchange I realized it was going to be a seriously long haul and increasingly difficult to make people believe we were each other. I mean, I have ZERO in common with koo-koo-ca-chew Ms. Pitt. The jig would be up, pronto.

Then I noticed Mr. Hudson approaching. Lately, Mr. Hudson was a familiar face in the halls of Burroughs Junior High. He was a substitute and I guess a lot of teachers had been out lately. And while his tie selection was nearly always unfortunate, his warm eyes overrode his taste in neckwear.

He had a little shy smile, and I knew exactly what that meant—it meant he must have a crush on Ms. Pitt. It was kind of crazy to think that teachers could have crushes like teenagers (and let's be honest, to have *lives* at all). I couldn't believe any man would be pining for Ms. Pitt, but then again, different strokes for different folks. I reached out and stopped him from passing.

"I had no idea you had such a crush!" I said it before I could stop myself.

Mr. Hudson looked down and muttered, getting a bit red in the face, "Well . . ."

It also became apparent that the Ms. Pitt–Mr. Hudson romance might need a little nudge. I always wanted to play matchmaker, something right out of *Fiddler on the Roof* or something, so I figured this was my shot. "And I have NEVER seen a teacher send anyone a Candy-Gram like that before. Very gutsy move. Very P.D.A."

Mr. Hudson's face clouded over. It was obvious he didn't follow that last part. Maybe this meddling wasn't such a keen idea—I did have bigger fish to fry. Like SWITCHING MY BODY BACK WITH MY TEACHER, for instance.

It took a minute to figure out what Ms. Pitt would say to him. "Well, I'd better ingest some healthful nutrients, Mr. H!" I *knew* that was wrong, so I blazed out of there just as I thought I heard Mr. Hudson say, "See you tonight . . . then." But I didn't even stop to think what that might mean.

CHAPTER 6

I Scotch-taped my class schedule to the inside of my locker so Ms. Pitt would know where to go. I mean, it was the least I could do—I wasn't about to have my grades slide any more by this body-switching business.

And I admit—and I am surprised to say this—it was a little satisfying.

Now Ms. Pitt would REALLY see firsthand how mindless and antiquated home ec was (it was required, don't ask), how dull earth science was, and also how Mr. Rendell blinked unnaturally while teaching social studies. It was as if he was constantly blinking dust out of his eyes and it was completely distracting. Who could focus on how the legislative branch works with that going on?

I was glad it was finally lunch and I could refuel—seriously, this whole switching bodies thing was beyond draining and I needed some nourishment. I looked out at the lunchroom cafeteria, scanning for Hadley or Soup or Nan. I couldn't spot them. Instead I saw Zane silently munching on a sandwich and I sighed longingly. Even the sight of him reaching for a Frito was intoxicating. But when the science teacher Ms. Kenkel heard this audible sigh, she shot Ms. Pitt a puzzled look.

"Headed into the teachers' lounge, then?" Ms. Kenkel asked in a suspicious tone.

"Oh. Yeah. Teachers' lounge, right. The fortress," I joked. Ms. Kenkel held the door open for me and I crept inside.

I had always wondered what lay behind these doors. What were the teachers talking about in here? Major school secrets? Lurid gossip? I wouldn't be surprised if there was a shrine to Tatum up on the walls.

Instead, I was amazed to see a TV blaring *Days of Our Lives*. Two of the teachers were riveted to the TV.

"*Whoever gave her that medication wanted her to lose her mind,*" a very earnest handsome soapy star on TV said to a woman lying in a hospital bed.

I burst into laughter—somehow a soap opera seemed strangely removed from the intention of higher learning. (And I use the term "higher learning" loosely.) "Soap operas? Seriously?"

The only response to this was the volume being turned up.

I walked to the refrigerator and opened it up. I found several cans of Slim Fast and brown paper bags. There was also an environmentally friendly recyclable lunch box that had clearly been marked with a Sharpie: MS. PITT. Of course. I reached for it and sat down . . . all this body-switching had made me ravenous.

I was horrified (and not surprised) to see Ms. Pitt had packed a weird organic vegan mush thing. I didn't even know what it was. All I knew was that it was very suspicious-looking lying there in the Tupperware bowl.

"Gross!" I said aloud, and Ms. Kenkel shot me another worried look.

"Well . . . that's what I've been saying for years. I've never known how you do it," Ms. Kenkel said. "With all the organic this and organic that, that is."

"Me neither." I got up and tossed the food into the garbage. Ms. Kenkel let out a shocked gasp but was clearly amused. Then I went straight to the vending machine. I dumped a few quarters in and whammo, a yummy Dolly Madison fruit pie fell at my feet. I decided to top it off with a little Mountain Dew. That was more like it.

Several teachers looked at me like I had just tossed a box full of kittens out of the window or something.

"What?" I addressed their collective disbelief through a big mouthful of cherry pie. I then noticed the shop teacher, Mr. Krupp, asleep on the couch, snoring away. It also seemed Mrs. Silsand—who clearly was entirely too focused on *Days of Our Lives*—was GRADING English papers! Just blithely half reading papers and marking them up with a red A+ or B– or D+. The whole situation seemed profoundly half-baked.

"So guess how many hours it took to grade my papers last night," Ms. Kenkel asked with an air of familiarity as she chewed into her icky-looking tuna salad sandwich. I was clueless.

"Thirty minutes? An hour?" I asked.

Ms. Kenkel burst into hysterics. "Good one."

I looked over again at Mrs. Silsand's checked-out grading. I gestured toward her and whispered, "It's not taking Mrs. Silsand long."

"Maybe that's the secret. . . . I admit: Sometimes I wish I cared less. But I do care. And I know you get that more than anyone else." She smiled at me and I gave a little understanding grin back. Ms. Pitt *was* dedicated, I couldn't deny that. "Three and a half hours."

I couldn't believe what I was hearing. "No way! *Three and a half? HOURS?* At night? To grade papers?"

Ms. Kenkel's eyes grew quizzical. "Well, don't act so surprised."

"EVERY NIGHT?" I still couldn't believe it—I never even considered the fact that it took any teacher any time at all to grade or correct papers or tests. I thought maybe it all happened magically . . . or through osmosis . . . or . . .

"I know. And meanwhile, we haven't gotten a pay raise in what . . . four years?"

"That is just so very, very wrong," I stated.

"Tell me something I don't know. So. Did you hear about Ed?" Ms. Kenkel said conspiratorially, leaning in, as if sharing a juicy secret.

"Ed?" *Edward Scissorhands? Ed Norton? Ed who?*

"Ed Wells, of course."

"Principal Wells?!" Oh, this was going to be good.

"You feeling okay today?" Ms. Kenkel placed a clammy hand on my forehead, as if checking my temperature.

"Actually, I'm not feeling entirely like myself, no." I smiled. It was the truth. "But I'm fine."

"Well, I heard Judy—"

"Judy?" Again, I needed the CliffsNotes.

"Judy, Ed's *wife*?"

"Of course, right. His wife. Judy. Go on."

"Well . . . Apparently she's been 'on a trip.'" Ms. Kenkel

provided awkward and a bit too theatrical air quotes. "For about three months now. No one's seen her anywhere at school, in town, in church—she just has virtually '*disappeared*,'" she whispered, and again did some more air quotes. Who she was quoting, I wasn't sure. "Now, don't you just think that's the strangest thing?"

"Maybe she likes to travel," I offered.

"Yes . . . to divorce court!" Ms. Kenkel clucked and laughed uproariously at her big joke. It was like she thought she was channeling Chris Rock. "You know I'm feeling just crazy enough today to admit something, Carol."

"Carol?" Oh, right, Carol. I just gulped down my fruit pie and nodded as if to suggest "Go on, please." This could be interesting.

"Well," she started tentatively. "I have always been so jealous of you."

"Jealous?" Of Ms. Pitt? I mean . . . of *me*? "Good grief, why?"

"Because you really seem to speak the kids' language."

Chunks of my Dolly Madison cherry pie almost went everywhere. "Speak their language?! You've got to be kidding!"

"No . . . I'm not." Ms. Kenkel seemed to be a wee bit irritated now.

"Why, because I use the term 'jiggy'? Oh, please! P.S.: No one uses 'jiggy' anymore." I laughed.

Ms. Kenkel seemed a bit indignant and went to the refrigerator to snoop around. She leaned into it, inspecting the contents and displaying her rather rotund backside. I felt guilty about what I'd said about 'jiggy'—it was really dismissive.

"But, uh . . . thanks," I offered.

Her only response was a cluck. I realized I should use this lounge time to find out what teachers really think of me . . . but I didn't want to make them too suspicious.

"Say," I ventured, trying to sound as breezy-casual as possible, "what do you think of Hadley and Tatum Fox?"

Ms. Kenkel stood up and turned, adjusting her shirt awkwardly. "You mean the former student Tatum Fox?"

I nodded. She turned around and went back to her fridge inspection. "Tatum Fox was a delight. A gem. A ray of sunshine, truly."

I looked down at my Dolly Madison fruit pie wrapping, defeated.

"Few students radiate like that girl. Few people. In

fact, I've never known anyone quite like her. And gorgeous, good grief! You couldn't help but stare!" She paused reminiscing. "We sure do miss her."

I couldn't take it anymore. I didn't even stay to hear what she thought of me. Who needed it? I bolted.

CHAPTER 7

Just as I exited the teacher's lounge with a strong desire to flee coursing through my body (or . . . Ms. Pitt's body I guess is more accurate), I ran smack into myself. I mean Hadley. I mean Ms. Pitt.

This was the most confusing day of my life. Seriously, I felt like I might spontaneously implode at any moment.

"We need to speak to a healer," Hadley said breathlessly.

"A *healer*? No, no . . . we need something WAY beyond the self-help aisle for this weirdness," I asserted.

"But obviously our souls are confused and we need some metaphysical guidance! I know lots of people who would be happy to help," Hadley pleaded.

"Look—all I want is to switch back. . . . I'm really not in the mood to talk to those freaky-deaky, your-aura-is-violet friends of yours!"

"They're not freaky-deaky." She paused, obviously

stung. "And do you honestly think I don't desperately want to switch back, too? You *seriously* think I want to jeopardize my big interview today?" said Hadley. "So. I'm ready for *your* brilliant suggestions, since mine seem to be so substandard and 'freaky-deaky.'"

"I have no idea." It was the unfortunate truth. I truly was clueless. It was possible I could spend the rest of my days with a closet full of peasant skirts.

Hadley narrowed her eyes a bit and said, "Teaching is harder than it looks, isn't it?"

"Yeah. I'll grant you that. But thank goodness Zane wheeled in that DVD player. I had your classes watch CNN all period."

"Why?"

"I didn't know what else to do!" Standing up in front of a class of eighth graders made me realize teaching was harder than it looked. We paused, uncertain how to proceed. I mean, seriously, how do you go about switching bodies back with someone? You don't know either? Exactly my point.

Across the hall Milly waved and then pointed to her watch.

"Oh. You Rock! Self Matters! There's a meeting now," Hadley said with a serious lack of enthusiasm. "You're the chairperson."

"I am?"

"Yup." Hadley took my arm and made me wave back to Milly. I then put up a finger to indicate I'd be there in a second. "It's in the library."

"You sure do head up a lot of groups, huh?" I asked.

"Four of them."

"Why so many, Ms. Pitt?" I almost felt bad for her.

"Because." Hadley paused. "I'd do anything for you kids."

For a moment, I was truly taken aback.

I touched Hadley's arm and nodded my head. "I know." It was so strange—here I was in the adult's body but I felt compelled to take care of the actual adult, Ms. Pitt! It seemed like I *was* becoming the adult after all.

"We'll figure it out. For now I've got a . . . Rock Yourself . . . You Matter—"

"You Rock! Self Matters!" Hadley corrected.

"Right. I have a meeting to hit," I said, and went to join Milly and her probably too-upbeat supporters. *Please tell me Kaya Tisch won't be there.* It would be entirely too much sunniness for my delicate system.

I figured we'd talk about our Feelings with a capital *F* and I'd slather their self-esteem with some positive reinforcement. If I told Milly I liked her jean jacket, I'm sure that would be enough. . . .

Because I REALLY had to get back to the business of figuring out the big switchback-eroo.

The library was garishly lit and the walls were covered with those lame posters celebrating Earth Day and seasons and literary figures. Milly had some chairs set up in a circle and a meager few students had shown up to pay homage to their all-important teenage self-esteem.

"Ms. Pitt!" Milly announced with a super smile. "We're running a bit late today."

"Well, sorry, gang. It's been a weird day. . . . Seriously, you have no idea." I sat down and managed a smile to the few in attendance. And they all just stared back blankly in response. Crickets. It was obvious I was not getting Ms. Pitt's style right.

I realized I had no idea what to say, despite the fact that I knew all too well the precarious internal shelf on which self-esteem balanced. However, I was also sane enough to realize that sitting in a circle in the library with Milly Albright and friends was NOT going to help me feel one ounce better. Or make me feel more confident about having a supermodel-to-be for an older sister.

"So," Milly offered, trying to get the self-worth ball rolling. "What's on the agenda today?"

"Well," I heard myself say, "I guess . . . you should

just go ahead and recap last week's meeting, Milly. How about that? Cool?"

"Okay . . . I can do that." Milly seemed a little suspicious when she reached into her backpack and pulled out a balloon.

I almost had to laugh. "What—did you all make balloon animals?"

Milly looked crushed. "No! This balloon is a metaphor for the fragile self-esteem of the average teenager."

"You're serious?"

"It was YOUR idea. And it made a lot of sense to me." Milly looked down, embarrassed and confused. I instantly felt horrible, like I was stomping on poor Milly's self-esteem and squashing it to pieces.

"So . . . tell me again how it works."

With that, Milly rebounded with enthusiasm. She blew up the balloon, taking big deliberate breaths. When the balloon was full, she displayed it proudly.

"This is positive self-esteem. Full and complete."

Milly let some air creep out of the balloon, causing a slow *hiss*. "And when other people say negative things about you, they affect your self-esteem and cause it to leak away."

"Oh, now I get it!" I blurted. Everyone stared

quizzically. Right, right. I should know this information already.

Milly continued. "Like, take me. Last week I was feeling okay about myself. Not great, but okay. Normal, at least . . . and then something happened. I went to see my brother Trey's baseball game. I mean, he's the pitcher at high school and he's all cool and everything. . . . He drives a Jetta." Murmurs of acknowledgment . . . Jettas *are* terrifically awesome. "And I'm really proud of him . . . and if he's cool, maybe somehow I am, too, you know? So I was really excited. I wanted everyone to know that the star pitcher was MY brother. I even wore a button with his picture on it and a jersey of his. You know, to show support," Milly said, her voice on the verge of cracking. You just knew this wasn't going to be good. "And when Jake Hinkle asked my brother if I was his sister and pointed to me, Trey saw me in the stands, you know, with my dorky sign and stupid button on, wearing his jersey, and he said no. He shook his head and told him no. That I was not his sister." She paused and couldn't continue.

Instead, she just released the air of the balloon and it all hissed out until it was empty, a limp plastic strip in her hand. No one said a thing and tears welled in Milly's eyes.

"He said I wasn't his sister," she softly repeated.

It was tragic and every fiber of my being related to her story—of wanting to be cool by association, of feeling like the lame consolation prize of the family, of despair. I guess the day was already a bit on the dramatic side and this Milly episode unleashed an emotional beast within me.

I felt tears springing to my eyes (or, technically, Ms. Pitt's eyes, but it was my Hadley heart that was feeling this so intensely). "God, that is just so awful, Milly. I'm just really really sorry." I had to cover my face as the tears were coming so fast.

The other kids looked at me as if I had sprung a second head—I guess Ms. Pitt didn't usually weep in the Truth Circle.

"I can also really relate to what you're saying," I managed.

"You can?"

I looked Milly dead in the eye. *"More than you'll ever know,"* I said with total genuineness. "Thanks for having the courage to tell the truth today. We all should be so brave." My voice cracked on that last part.

Milly was a bit confused by this turn but I did sense she felt validated. I snagged the balloon out of her hand

and blew it up with a vengeance. Soon the balloon was a happy red orb again, suggesting children's parties and proms, not woeful self-esteem.

"This was MY self-esteem last week. Let me tell you what happened. I could just die. . . . I was in between classes and in a rush, especially between third and fourth period, because the classes were on opposite sides of the school. Anyway, I'm dashing down and I completely have to pee. Like, I won't be able to concentrate at all unless I hit the bathroom, you know? So I bolt into the john, do what I do, and dash out." I'm really getting into this story.

"But why would you have to dash to the opposite side of the school? You teach all day in room fourteen B, right?" Milly asked.

Oh. Right. "Well, I had to pick something up from Mrs. Bird."

This seemed to make everyone feel a whole lot better, despite the holes in logic.

"Anyway, I dash out of the bathroom and fly down the hall . . . and I can hear some people laughing, pointing, whatever. Which on some level I'm completely used to. But the laughs are getting louder and I realize it's directed at me. No shock, right? And that's when I realize that MY SKIRT HAS BEEN TUCKED INTO MY

UNDERWEAR AND I'VE BEEN MOONING THE ENTIRE SCHOOL."

To punctuate this story, I let all the air out of the balloon and let it deflate in my hand.

Gasps of no! chorused the library.

"Oh, *and* I'm wearing lame-o days-of-the-week underwear. Wednesday is on full display!"

"NO!"

"Oh, yeah. And I had to do this in front of Zane Henderson, can you believe it?"

"Um . . . Why would Zane Henderson matter so much?" Paul Canaan asked pointedly.

Oh, right. Teachers don't usually tell stories like this. And teachers aren't supposed to have crushes on their thirteen-year-old students. . . . "He doesn't, I guess. I'm just saying . . . Anyway, it was awful. Just awful."

"It's kind of weird that we didn't hear anything about it," Milly said as if she didn't quite believe me.

"I think I heard something about Hadley Fox doing that," a rigid boy stated.

There was silence. Milly cleared her throat. "Everything that is spoken in the Truth Circle is valued and true." She looked over at me. "That sounds *so* embarrassing, Ms. Pitt."

I locked eyes with Milly and felt—as Oprah as this sounds—our souls connecting. Like we really saw each other. It just felt natural to get up and offer her a hug. On cue, Milly stood up, too, and we embraced, like old war veterans who hadn't seen each other for years.

"I apologize if I haven't been as nice to you as I could be," I whispered to Milly.

"Oh, Ms. Pitt, you're the best! You're always SO nice!"

I smiled. "I am, aren't I?"

At that very moment, Mr. Wells was passing by the library and managed to get a glimpse of this lovefest through the door window.

I hugged Milly again, really holding her, trying to relay my earnestness. "It's time we all stop wearing the masks and start talking the TRUTH," I heard myself say, voice cracking. Okay, I admit the weirdness and stress of today was making me more than a little bit unstable.

I wasn't letting go. At all. I was clinging to her like she was my life vest. And this bear hug may have been a BIT too much for Milly. She looked at the other incredulous students and gestured with her eyes that this had migrated into a weird territory. Milly tried to pull away but I held on for dear life, clinging to her for reasons I'm not sure even I understood.

Mr. Wells entered the library. "Ms. Pitt. Might I have a word with you?"

I finally pulled away and Milly looked relieved. "A word?"

"My office. Now." He turned and left, and I knew I had to follow.

CHAPTER 8

I sat Ms. Pitt's posterior down into a seat across from Mr. Wells and peered around the room. The room's greatest offense was definitely bad decor. Think fake wood paneling and lots of plaques and diplomas up on the wall. A few photos of Mr. Wells shaking hands with men in bad suits. Plus weird pictures of pointy-nosed creatures. His pet gerbils? The "Trust" and "Honesty" posters with the ubiquitous eagles and shots of mountain streams didn't help the overall effect.

Regardless, being in the principal's office was terrifying. I had worked so hard my whole life to avoid this exact spot and now I was here—IN MY TEACHER'S BODY!

It was anxiety inducing, to say the least.

Mr. Wells stared at me with angry slits for eyes. I have no idea what Ms. Pitt had done prior to this to make him so hostile.

"Ms. Pitt," he started. I guess I didn't respond imme-diately—after all, it's not my name. I stared blankly for a second and snapped to.

"What? Oh. Yeah?"

"This morning I have seen you in two different cir-cumstances in which you were acting decidedly . . . *off*." He took his time with the "off."

"Yeah, well . . . it's been a rough morning." Which was the biggest understatement of the year, I thought bit-terly.

"Are you particularly nervous about the English department interview today? Perhaps that is jangling your nerves?" I know he wanted to sound diplomatic and concerned, but he was mostly suspicious.

"The interview is the least of my problems, trust me," I said.

"*Is it?*"

A weird silence followed, which was broken by a small tap on the door. Mr. Wells wasn't used to being inter-rupted, that was obvious. "Yes?"

Mr. Hudson opened the door a crack and popped his head in. He gave a nice smile to me and I thought he had such sweet eyes. Or maybe that was just in comparison to Mr. Wells's snakelike stare.

"Hey there. Sorry to interrupt . . . but I just wanted to

make sure everything was okay in here."

"I'm having a chat with Ms. Pitt. Does this concern you?"

"Well, you see . . ." Mr. Hudson got red in the face again. It was kind of adorable. "Not really. No. I guess it doesn't concern me directly but I had heard, you know, that Ms. Pitt was having a bad day and a little stressed and that you wanted to see her . . ."

Mr. Wells was about to explode but Mr. Hudson continued with his rambling explanation. "And I just wanted to say that for the record, Ms. Pitt is a terrific teacher."

"I'm sure Ms. Pitt appreciates your vote of confidence, but this is a private matter between Ms. Pitt and myself. Thank you."

Mr. Hudson had no choice but to close the door. He gave a heartfelt little grin on his way out. At least *some* adults were civil!

"It seems you have a loyal following, Ms. Pitt." Mr. Wells smiled, but it wasn't a nice smile at all. "Is there anything wrong, anything you'd like to discuss or share . . . a grievance or concern?"

"Not particularly . . ." I think he'd be happy if I admitted I like the taste of bat blood or something—he WANTED something tragic or a big admission on my part.

"You've always struck me as an . . . *emotional person*—"

"Is that a bad thing?" Ms. Pitt was emotive, sure, but it wasn't like she was a bad person, which was the serious undertone of this conversation.

"Not necessarily, but a propensity for emotion can lead to uneven teaching styles."

Uneven teaching styles? How mean was that?

He just half smiled and I felt my temples pound. He was like a cat with a mouse and he wanted to pounce, it was clear. . . .

"Mr. Wells, please, what do you really want to say to me?!" My voice was cracking and I was teetering on the edge. I didn't know who (whom?) I felt worse for, Ms. Pitt or myself.

"It just seems that perhaps of late you have been more than uneven, Ms. Pitt. You seem . . . scattered. Spread. Too. Thin."

With that, the dam broke.

"You know what? Maybe I *am* spread too thin! Maybe I *do too much*! I mean, have you ever had six hours of homework in one night? No?! I didn't think so!"

Now Mr. Wells was REALLY nervous.

"Do you know that having a 4.0 isn't *enough* to get into an Ivy League school anymore? You have to get a 4.5

or a 4.6 and basically be a genetic freak? You think Stanford cares if you're on the softball team? Oh no! You have to be *captain* of the softball team *and* translate books for the blind *and* speak nine languages AND—"

Mr. Wells was beyond freaked. "All right, this is confounding—"

"Confounding? Oh, you think you know confounding? No, no—you don't know confounding like I know confounding. . . . Because me and *confounding*?! We go way back." I felt a little bit of spittle on my lip from this crazed outburst. I stopped just short of telling him what was the most confounding of all (answer: switching bodies with your eighth-grade English teacher).

Mr. Wells ran his hand over his head, slicking back his hair, totally unnerved. He looked down as if to regain his composure. "Ms. Pitt. Frankly, you are not making any sense. I would like you to please go home at once to get some rest. And if I were you, I would definitely reschedule that interview."

I tried to take some deep breaths but wasn't exactly successful.

There was a small knock at the door. It did not open but behind it, I heard Mr. Hudson's hesitant voice: "If you need a ride . . ."

Mr. Wells's eyes rolled and he gestured to the door.

It was clear he wanted me to leave and fast. So I did just that.

I ran smack into Mr. Hudson and smiled at him gratefully. "Thanks so much for the offer. And thanks, too, for the cool words."

"I meant it. Now. You should really take a break. I'll go get my car and pull on up." Before I could say anything, he was off.

I had to admit, getting out of school and its strangeness would be a good thing. Maybe then we could get more active with finding a solution for this body switch . . . I had to track down Hadley.

I scanned the cafeteria, searching for myself, which is an entirely bizarre thing to do. Instead, I saw Zane and whatever panic I felt melted a bit. . . . Just the sight of him always caused an internal sigh. And it seemed he was headed my way!

I took a big calming breath.

"Hey, Zane! What's up?" I said way too singsongy.

"Um . . . nothing much," he responded with absolute perfect delivery.

"Cool, cool. So can we take a rain check on that tutoring? Because I am psyched to hang out . . . but I gotta blaze home early."

Zane looked a bit puzzled and I realized the term *blaze*

was probably not in Ms. Pitt's vocabulary. "I mean . . . head home . . . Because my cat's sick. Not that I'm this crazy cat person. I'm not."

"Okay . . . So will the, uh, tutoring obviously help with my grade, then?"

I leaned in, smiling. "Absolutely . . ." And then what I said just came out like verbal diarrhea: "You're only, like, the most A-plus person I know."

Zane took off.

Not that I blame him . . . but I couldn't help myself, I had never had so much contact with Zane before. Being near him scrambled my brain and made me completely inappropriate!

CHAPTER 9

I stood outside the school waiting for my ride. I looked down at my watch, and boy oh boy, Ms. Pitt had really taken the natural-world obsession too far—the hands of her watch were lame-o butterfly wings. I'm all for self-renewal metaphors and all, but the butterfly motif was so cheesy and obvious.

Where was Mr. Hudson? He sure was taking some sweet time getting his car to drive me home. After my meltdown, I was more than anxious to get the heck out of Dodge. Every fiber and inch of my being wanted to escape. NOW.

I couldn't believe it when I saw Tatum's Accord pull up out of the corner of my eye. Surely this insane day was playing with my brain—Tatum wouldn't be at school to get me now—I mean, school wasn't even out yet! But I turned my head and it was definitely her. She slammed into the curb and screeched the car to a halt.

And she was sobbing. Her shoulders were shaking and tears were streaming down her beautiful raccoon-streaked face. I instantly ran up to her car, and Tatum looked embarrassed, started wiping away her tears and putting on a brave face.

I tapped on her window and she rolled it down.

"Oh, hey, Ms. Pitt," she said with a froggy voice.

Ms. Pitt?! No, no—I'm your SISTER! Your FRIEND!

"What's going on? What's wrong?" I asked breathlessly.

Tatum blew her nose forcefully. Even though it was a serious honk, she made it sound adorable and only added to her charm. She was one of those impossibly enchanting people who can burp and everyone giggles. "Sorry. It's just . . . a really bad day," she explained, and started to cry again.

"Yeah, and I sorta figured that part out!" I exclaimed. Tatum's face clouded over with confusion—I guess teachers aren't really encouraged to play in the sarcasm sandbox. How I wanted to tell her I had switched places with Ms. Pitt! But I had the distinct feeling that would be entirely too much information and send Tatum over the edge. She needed sanity right now. "Sorry. I mean, just tell me what's wrong."

Tatum looked down and her chin quivered. I had *never*

seen Tatum so distraught before. Then a thought crashed into my head: "It's not Mom or Dad, is it?"

She gave me a puzzled look. "No, my family's fine. . . ."

I wanted to say *Except for your sister!* but I tried to sound as rational as embrace-the-universe Ms. Pitt. "Then what is it?"

"I'm sorry you have to see me like this . . . but of any teacher, you're the one who I'd feel most comfortable melting down in front of. So . . . yah for me." Tatum gave a sad little "woo-hoo" gesture. "I found out . . . that . . . I didn't get into Colorado State today."

"Oh no, Tatum! Your last choice!"

"How did you know?"

I smiled unconvincingly. "A feeling, I guess . . . Maybe Hadley said something. Anyway, go on."

"I was in the library and looked up my acceptance online. And there in my in-box was a big fat rejection e-mail. 'Thank you very much for your interest in Colorado State, but we will not be accepting your application at this time.'" She paused, shaking her head miserably. "I mean, I didn't even want to go to Colorado State! I'm sure Fort Collins is nice enough . . . but . . . I thought I'd get in there *easy*!"

"Oh, Tatum, I'm so sorry. So so sorry." I wanted to hug her but that would probably freak her out completely.

"If I was more like Hadley, I wouldn't be in this situation, which is totally screwed."

What she said jumped out at me. "More like *Hadley*?"

"You know, Hadley's got it figured out, and she studies so hard and is so brilliant. . . . But I guess I learned my lesson a little too late, huh?"

I was stunned—*I* had it figured out? Really?

"Let's face it, no college wants the homecoming queen who gets Ds in math. . . ." said Tatum. And with that, her head fell and she started to really sob again.

"Oh, Tatum . . . I can't stand to see you like this!"

"I can't stand to be like this! This . . . this . . . blubbering joke!" She looked at her sad reflection in the visor mirror. "You know, everyone thinks my life is perfect but it's not. I'm a joke. I'm an idiot." She said it with convincing self-loathing, and I had never heard Tatum so down before. "Everyone makes allowances for me."

It had never occurred to me that Tatum could feel this way.

"Even Brad. We're totally not getting along," Tatum went on.

"BRAD?! You and Brad? But Brad's the bomb!" Brad was only the single hottest guy at high school. He was like that New England Patriots quarterback, but cuter (if that's possible).

Tatum gave a creeped-out look. "Anyway, I'm sure he'll be *much* more likely to break up with me now that I'm junior college–bound. After all, Brad got early acceptance into Michigan . . . but then again, he also got a 720 on his math SATs. Unlike me who got, like, a four."

"Oh, Tatum, you did not get a four."

"Okay, a five. Maybe I could train to become a valet parker. Or I could work at the mall. You know, hand out free samples of Cinnabons for the rest of my life . . . I'd be good at that. Ughh . . . I'm so pathetic." She started to cry again and looked at her watch. She was startled. "Wait, what am I doing here? School's not even out yet! I freaked out so much that I just bolted!"

"Maybe you should come to the nurse's office." I knew my offer wouldn't be welcome but it was something.

"Go to the junior high nurse? Okay, now I'm *really* having a crisis. No . . . I gotta get out of here. Tell Hadley to get a ride from someone else, okay?" She sounded sketchy and wasn't making the most sense. I saw her hands were shaking.

"Seriously, Tatum, you shouldn't be driving."

"I gotta go, gotta go, gotta go. Sorry, Ms. Pitt!" With that, she erratically drove off. I halfheartedly tried to run after her but her Accord sped off like a comet. She even drove up onto the sidewalk on the way out.

"Oh, boy."

This was big information. I had to do something to help Tatum. . . . I had never seen her like this and she shouldn't be driving, it was true. But mostly I was obsessing over the fact that Tatum's life was *not* perfect. And was it my imagination, or did she actually sound strangely envious . . . of . . . *me*?

CHAPTER 10

I stood there, dazed, absorbing this bizarre news.

First, I was standing, in Ms. Pitt's body, outside of my junior high blinking confusedly into the sun.

Weird.

Then, I had just heard my mythically, genetically, spectacularly beautiful sister say she was envious of ME.

Me with the flat chest and straw hair and nonexistent social life.

Doubly weird.

But Tatum was also in trouble, that was clear. She was a wreck and that was putting it mildly. She should NOT be behind the wheel.

Then I felt a hand practically strangle me from behind. I turned to see *myself* tackling me. Talk about a lucid nightmare.

"I heard you're being sent home early," Hadley said

breathlessly. "Why? Did you lose control in front of Mr. Wells?"

"Chill, okay?! So I had a mini-meltdown! But considering the circumstances, I think I'm entitled!" I did have a point. "Mr. Hudson volunteered to drive you home. He totally digs you, by the way."

I could see a bumbling Mr. Hudson out of the corner of my eye, calling, "One minute! Be there in one minute!"

Hadley silenced the thought. "I'd never get involved with a fellow teacher."

"You should. You're at school most of the time, anyway," I pointed out.

"I'm going to meet Mr. Right at yoga or the health food store or . . ." Hadley faded off.

There was a pregnant beat and I knew that yoga classes and health food stores probably weren't teeming with loads of single guys for Ms. Pitt to meet.

But I had to get back to the matter at hand. Or, *matters* at hand, actually. "Look, something's come up. I know my sister, Tatum, is a favorite student of yours and the rest of the civilized world, let's be honest. Anyway, she was just here and she's really freaking out. I've never ever seen her like that."

"What's wrong?"

"She didn't get into Colorado State. It was her last choice and she was a wreck, having an early existential crisis. She practically crashed her car when she drove off—"

"*Crashed her car?!*"

"I know, that's why we have to help her. She could hurt someone or herself. We need to team up to help Tatum."

Hadley just nodded solemnly and I knew we were committed. We may have had zero idea how to help ourselves and get unswitched, but we could unite to aid Tatum.

Mr. Hudson ran up, completely red in the face. "My Chevy Malibu won't start." He looked down, humiliated. "As if driving a Chevy Malibu isn't embarrassing enough."

Hadley really laughed at that one and I was pleased— it was about time Ms. Pitt woke up to the possibility of Mr. Hudson. He was what my grandma would call a "good egg."

That's when the thought hit me! I'm in Ms. Pitt's body, and she's easily mid-thirties and has been driving for years—

Hadley didn't see it coming.

I reached into Ms. Pitt's purse and yanked out her keys, bolting for her car, a funky little Prius. It hummed to life (literally—those hybrids are so quiet it's almost unnerving) and I put the pedal to the metal (and for the record, hybrids *can* move). I tore up and screeched to a halt in front of a horrified Hadley and Mr. Hudson. My face hurt I was smiling so huge.

I was *driving*!!!

"You can't drive! Get out *now*!" Hadley screeched.

But I just love it when you have facts on your side. "Fine. Do you have *your* license, *Hadley*?"

She was caught. Mr. Hudson shook his head in general confusion, which seemed to be a theme.

"Mr. Hudson, you have to drive," Hadley stammered.

Mr. Hudson was so turned around he barely knew how to respond. "But—"

"Trust me on this one. You drive." Hadley was insistent. "Neither one of us should be behind the wheel today."

She had a point there. "How do you feel about a little adventure, Mr. Hudson?" I asked him with a grin and threw him the car keys.

"Why not?" Mr. Hudson smiled back at me (or should I say, smiled back at Ms. Pitt. His eyes were warm and I just knew he had it bad for her). "And it's Randy."

"Right, right, Randy." I could tell Mr. Hudson—or Randy—was shocked by how bold Ms. Pitt was being. He liked this attention.

Everyone climbed into the Prius. "We have to find my sister, Tatum," I said.

"Your . . . sister?" Mr. Hudson asked.

"I mean . . . *my* sister. She's in trouble and we need to calm her down," Hadley said.

"But . . . what about your big interview today? Shouldn't you get some rest?" Mr. Hudson asked with concern. "Weren't you told to—"

"I can't rest until I know Tatum's okay," I said with utmost sincerity.

Mr. Hudson considered for a moment. "And that's exactly why you're the amazing teacher that you are," he said, and Hadley audibly "aaahed" in response!

"That's sweet," Hadley offered, and Mr. Hudson smiled back.

"You just always think of everyone else before yourself, don't you?" he said.

I realized it was probably true—and it was also why she couldn't wake up to the fact that this great guy was vying for her attention.

"Let's head to my house—er, Hadley's house—and

see if Tatum is there," I said, and we headed off. We filled Mr. Hudson in on what Tatum was so destroyed about, and I wasn't surprised he knew who Tatum was. Jeez, even subs were getting fed on the mythology of Tatum!

CHAPTER 11

We pulled up in front of our house and I was so grateful that Mom would be at her pottery class. (Mom believed wholeheartedly in continually improving one's self, which meant she took a lot of classes, and our house was always littered with fairly terrible oil paintings and attempts at calligraphy and the like.) Regardless, I did NOT want to explain why I had brought two teachers to the house to look for her beyond-distraught golden daughter.

"I'll go to Tatum's room," I said. By Mr. Hudson's puzzled eyes, I guess he didn't think a teacher would necessarily know where a student's room was in the house. "I've been to the house for dinner," I said as if to explain. "You both blanket the rest of the house."

We took off like bloodhounds in pursuit. Hadley whispered, "I'll check your room." Meaning, MY room. Oh, this day . . .

Hadley bounded up the stairs with the agility and

spryness of a Disney woodland creature. When she reached the top of the stairs, she sailed down them again with a huge grin on her face.

"I can't believe how *fabulous* and *light* and *lithe* I feel!" Hadley chirped to me. "Seriously, your body is so spry and lightweight, it practically trots itself around! And no aches and pains, it's fantastic! Uh—if only yoga made me feel this way!" Hadley did a little playful shadowboxing and bopped about.

It was all a bit much and I put a hand on her head, silencing the bounce. "Why don't you hop on up to my room, then?" I asked.

Hadley nodded and ran up the stairs, entering my room. I chased after her. She was right about those aches and pains.

I could tell Ms. Pitt was eager to see a teenager's actual surroundings. She was acting like Jane Goodall, but instead of observing silverback gorillas, she was getting to see teenagers in their natural habitats.

And my room *is* fantastically organized for a teenager. My desk is obviously the fulcrum of the room and it's meticulously structured. Desk light, check. Ample supply of pens, check. Well-worn dictionary, check. All the tools were in plain sight that explained my drive and devotion to studies. I doubt that surprised Ms. Pitt one iota.

I heard a gasp. Ms. Pitt was clearly shocked by the rock band posters on the wall.

Immutable.

Sketched-Out Boy.

The IMs.

"Immutable?" she asked, pointing to the poster, perplexed.

"Oh, please don't admit you've never heard of Immutable?"

Hadley looked down, embarrassed, shaking her head no.

"They're huge! And all this time I thought you were so down with the teenage experience and everything. . . ." I ribbed.

"I thought . . . I really thought I was. . . ." I could see she really felt completely out of touch.

"Don't worry, Immutable's sort of fringe, anyway." Hadley exhaled and I knew she was relieved.

Just then, Mr. Hudson poked his head into the room.

Hadley put on a forced smile. "Any luck finding Tatum?"

"Nope. I don't think she's here," Mr. Hudson responded.

"Maybe Brad knows where she is. He's probably at tennis practice," I stated matter-of-factly.

"Brad?"

"Tatum's boyfriend. They're tight," I explained.

Mr. Hudson was in awe. "My God. When I said you were so in tune with the students, I had no idea! What are you, a mind reader?"

I gave Hadley a look and we smiled at each other and shook our heads. If you only knew, Mr. Hudson . . .

Hadley said, "Could we please have a moment alone?"

"Sure, I'll give you ladies a second. Be out waiting in the car." Mr. Hudson exited good-naturedly.

Hadley grabbed me. "We'd all be better off if we were back in our own bodies," she said. "Let's look up a solution quick on your computer. We haven't tried that yet."

I booted up my iMac and figured it was worth an investigation. I was willing to try anything.

We Googled "body switch" and started scanning. It was NOT reassuring.

"Here's 'body switching' at occultforums.com," Hadley read. We both shuddered.

"Pass," I said. "And links to body-switching movies. Not helpful."

"Okay, here's another," Hadley said. "'The Mind Body Switch Technique is the signature ability of the Yamanaka clan. With it, a ninja sends his mind into a target's body supplanting the target's mind with his own.'"

"So . . . we're either possessed or ninjas." A second passed and we both burst into hysterics. The whole situation was so absurd, you had to laugh. It was either that or lose your mind completely. Then again, maybe we already had. . . .

"Okay, focus. We have to focus," Hadley said, trying to regain composure. We waited another second and burst into more laughter.

"Come on," I said, wiping my eyes. "Clearly this is getting us nowhere. Let's get out of here."

We bolted for the car and jumped in, and I think we were both shocked by this bizarre crazy girly-giggling bonding. It was almost like we were kooky teenagers on the verge, and frankly the release felt good. I hadn't laughed that hard in a long time—even if it was psychotic. Maybe I had been studying too darn much and needed to smell the roses, not just the Wite-Out.

"Everything okay?" Mr. Hudson asked a bit suspiciously.

"Oh, sure. Don't mind us, we're just collectively losing our mind," Hadley said, and we practically had to bite our tongues to keep from laughing.

"So . . . where to?" Mr. Hudson asked as we pulled out.

"The high school. Let's check in with Tatum's boy-friend, Brad," I said.

We pulled into the high school parking lot, and, as usual, it piqued my interest. I mean, all the students drove. Well, not everyone, but from my vantage point, most drove cars. Talk about exotic. I would love that freedom. . . . To be practically an adult like these high school students, to go on dates and to drive? Or better yet—to be practically college-bound and almost free? Bring it on!

We parked the car near the tennis courts and went to find Brad. Brad and Tatum were usually attached at the hip. They were so the perfect couple that it was very nearly nauseating. Then again . . . Tatum had said they weren't getting along. Maybe everyone struggles and there is no perfect existence . . . although from my per-spective, it sure looked like Tatum was having the movie life. Maybe there *is* no movie life.

Brad was working on his serves, thunderously and meticulously slamming balls dead center to his imaginary opponent. He was tan and gorgeous, the consummate athlete. It was like Brad lived in different lighting, he was so divine.

We approached gingerly . . . Brad looked intent. I real-ized everyone was waiting for me to introduce our case, and I was the one who knew Brad. But I wasn't Hadley, I was Ms. Pitt. I elbowed Hadley to speak already.

"Uh, say, uh, Bob?" Hadley asked.

"*Brad!*" I whispered hotly.

"Brad?" she said again, and Brad turned. He was a total Greek god. He broke into a warm smile at the sight of me. How nice is that?

"Oh, hey, Hadley. How are ya?" Brad asked as he expertly dribbled his tennis ball in that very cool US Open way.

"Oh, don't ask," Hadley said, and she snuck a look at me. "Sorry to interrupt but it's urgent. You wouldn't happen to know where Tatum is, would you?"

"No. Why? Everything okay?" Now Brad stopped playing around with the tennis ball and seemed really concerned. Lord, he was dreamy. . . .

"Yeah. Should be fine. She's . . . well, I'm sure you'll find out soon enough. Just wondered if you know where she is, that's all. She was a little emotional before and I wanted to make sure she's okay," I said.

"Um . . . Who are you again?" Brad asked.

Oh, right. Brad has no idea who Ms. Pitt is! "I'm Ms. Pitt, her former teacher. And I'm sure you know more than anyone that it's easy to adore a girl like Tatum." I paused and looked right at Hadley and said quietly, "But then again, I adore all my students."

Hadley grinned back, and I think I saw her eyes glisten a little.

"Should I be worried?" Brad asked like the ultimate boyfriend. How could anything be wrong between them?

"I'm sure she'll be fine. Just want to track her down. Get back to your practice," I said. "Have Tatum call me—uh, Hadley's cell phone—if you hear from her, okay?"

Brad agreed and our unlikely trio moved on.

As we walked away from the tennis court, Mr. Hudson pulled me aside. Which is to say, he thought he pulled Ms. Pitt aside . . .

"Now, listen. You're doing the noble thing being worried about another student like this. But I have to get you to your interview now," Mr. Hudson said emphatically.

"Dude! No!" I said reflexively. "Which is to say . . . I can't," I said quietly. Hadley overheard this.

"Yes, it's probably not the best idea for Ms. Pitt to be going to that interview in her current state," Hadley said.

"Look, I believe in you. I know you're going through stress or something . . ." Mr. Hudson said.

"I'm freaky, right?" I asked.

"A bit. But the bottom line is you're the best person for the English chair position. You care about literature and how it can change lives. Instead of just about teaching for the tests, which is what they all want these days."

"Oh, Mr. Hudson," Hadley whispered with a bit too much emotion. I don't even think he heard her, which was lucky for all of us.

"Will you go to that interview, then? You're going to do great," Mr. Hudson asked. For a substitute teacher, he was pretty intense.

"How do you know?" I asked.

"Because you're *you*," Mr. Hudson responded.

I mean, seriously, how does a girl argue with that?

CHAPTER 12

The building where the school board met was sterile and drab, which seemed appropriate, as the school had such boring curriculums.

"This will end badly," Hadley said ominously, shaking her head.

"Come on, now! You know as well as anyone that Ms. Pitt is the right person for the position!" Mr. Hudson offered cheerfully.

"Remember that whole business with Principal Wells wanting me to leave school so I could rest? And suggesting I reschedule this interview?" I pointed out. "Not a good sign. At all."

"Oh, but what does Mr. Wells know? He raises pygmy hedgehogs."

I burst into laughter. "Shut! Up!"

Mr. Hudson was a little confused by that response from Ms. Pitt. "Surely you've seen his pictures, too?"

That explained the gerbils on his wall. Hadley asked, "Why would he do that?"

"Exactly. Raising pygmy hedgehogs alone proves his instability." Mr. Hudson chuckled. "Now go in there and wow 'em, Carol."

Hadley indicated she wanted a moment outside. I nodded and we excused ourselves, telling Mr. Hudson we'd get back to him in a sec. Really, his belief in Ms. Pitt was endearing but let's be realistic—I wasn't up for this interview! Ms. Pitt would lose the position for sure with *me* at the helm.

"Look," I said. "I know how much you want this chance but I do not want to blow it for you. I love books, sure, but heading the English department? On that, I *have not* done my homework. I blew one oral presentation today. Let's not make the body count two."

"Couldn't agree with you more," said Hadley.

"Okay, so we'll go in there and reschedule. Say you're not feeling well. . . . Mr. Wells can back you up on that one," I said. We agreed it was a plan: We'd figure out how to switch back, and *then* Ms. Pitt could do her big interview in her own body and with her own mind. Only then she could nail it.

I made sure we had my cell phone in case Tatum called, and we headed into the interview. United, we checked in with a receptionist who looked like she'd last smiled in 1975. A real Debbie Downer type. "May I help you?" she asked in a nasally voice.

"I'm Hadley—" I blurted. "I mean . . . I'm Ms. Pitt and this is Hadley Fox," I corrected, pointing to myself.

"We're here for the English department chair interview," said Hadley. "And we just need to talk to the committee to reschedule."

Debbie Downer's face scowled all the more at Hadley, which I didn't think was humanly possible. "But . . . why are you here? Aren't you a student?"

Hadley's face got red. "I am. I'm here for . . . support." There was a weird pause. "Go Ms. Pitt!" And that little rah-rah cheerleading move did not help the cause.

"And I'm not feeling well. Just ask Mr. Wells. I am so not up for this interview and I really need to reschedule. Totally for the best," I said.

Debbie reached for her phone and whispered into it gravely. After a moment, she returned the phone to its cradle. Whatever news she just heard on the phone, it seemed serious, based on her solemn expression. "You can take a seat if you'd like. They're not quite ready for you."

We sat down in the waiting area on the tacky vinyl chairs. The only reading material was *Auto Week*. Pass.

I wanted to just get this over with already. . . . We had to help Tatum and, more important, get our own bodies back.

Hadley stared up at the ceiling, biting her lip. Her brow was furrowed and she looked tortured.

"We'll get out of the interview, I promise," I said in an attempt to reassure her.

"I know. I was just so excited about this opportunity today," she said.

"Can I ask you something?" I took a deep breath. "Aren't you busy enough?" I asked. "I always see you at school running all over, chairing a zillion groups. Now you gotta go and run the entire English department, too?"

"I am involved. Maybe too involved, who knows? But . . . it means the world to me. I just don't want this rescheduling request to jeopardize my chance. That would *kill* me," she said gravely.

"But . . . why is it so important to you?"

She turned to me and stared at me earnestly with— unbelievably—*my eyes*. And I know myself. I meant business. "Because of Miss Mulligan."

Huh? "Miss Mulligan?"

"My eighth-grade English teacher. She opened up more for me than any other person I've ever met," she said.

"What was so special about her?" Now I had to know.

She took a breath. "Growing up, I always felt my parents liked their TV shows and newspapers more than they liked me. Which isn't a good way to feel. I was invisible, an intrusion in my own house. . . . But Miss Mulligan sure didn't make me feel that way. She listened to me and made me feel valued and important. You know—like a *person*! She gave me great books to read—phenomenal stuff like Whitman and *Franny & Zooey*—and then she wanted to know about my opinion. *My opinion!* She told me I was smart and I believed her."

I was amazed by her honesty. I also struggled to see Ms. Pitt as a teenager. . . . To me, she'd always been hippie-drippy Ms. Pitt and was probably born thirty-three years old. I was shocked to hear she had a life before teaching and that it wasn't all peaches and cream.

"Anyway, I vowed that if someday I could be a Miss Mulligan for someone, I would have done my job." She smiled to herself and I grinned back.

"I know you're a Miss Mulligan to my sister," I said. She looked at me with transparent longing, and I could tell she wanted me to say that I felt the same way about her. But I've always been a terrible liar, and the truth was, I *didn't* have the same feelings about Ms. Pitt that Tatum did.

"Well . . . I tried to be a Miss Mulligan for Tatum. At least that was always my intention when I set up those tutoring sessions for her," she said.

"Whoa, whoa—what?!" I asked. This was the first I'd ever heard about tutoring sessions. I saw Hadley's face redden and knew she instantly wanted to take that back.

"I shouldn't have said anything," she said.

I couldn't believe what I was hearing. "Tatum needed a tutor?"

"Oh, dear, I hope I didn't betray her confidence. But I could have sworn she said you knew about it. . . ."

I shook my head no.

"I know she was embarrassed. And it wasn't anything, really. Her comprehension skills were lacking, and I found her someone who could help, that's all."

"That's not 'just all.' I know English is her best subject. . . ."

She smiled. "It was *after* the tutoring. . . ."

I let this sink in. "So . . . isn't that enough, then?" I asked gently. "To know you make this sort of an impact?"

She thought about it for a moment—and let me tell you, it's strange to see yourself thinking when you yourself aren't even thinking! She continued, "It's just this . . . if I could head the English department, I would have much more control over the curriculum and steer the course load in a more enlightened route. This town can be so closed-minded, and I want to open their horizons just a crack."

I knew now was my time to let her know I *did* think she was a great teacher. And after today, I had to admit, it was *way* easier to recognize. "Well, you've got my vote," I said, and we grinned at each other.

"You can head in now," Debbie Downer said.

We entered the room and found Mr. Wells at the head of the table along with an assorted group of predictable suspects. Everyone on the committee looked like they'd climbed out of a Sears catalog from 1988—not exactly the most with-it-looking crowd. And Mr. Wells was *not* happy to see us enter. In fact, no one seemed very enthused by our entrance. . . . I had no doubt Mr. Wells had been poisoning the board's take on Ms. Pitt after today's craziness.

But all I could see when I looked at Mr. Wells now were his pygmy hedgehogs. Could a hobby be any more weird? And also, aren't hedgehogs small enough? Do you have to make them smaller?

"Now, Ms. Pitt, I had hoped you would get some rest after today's outburst," he said drily. "And why did you bring a student? Though we do wish all students could be more like Hadley Fox." He smiled.

Okay, even though he's a creepy principal who breeds hedgehogs, wishing students were more like me is still really good to hear, right?

"Oh, I can wait outside—" Hadley said.

"It's okay. We—*I*—just need to reschedule this interview and we'll both be on our way," I said. "And sorry about before, Mr. Wells. Today's been . . . well, odd doesn't begin to describe it. I haven't been feeling like myself," I said.

"To say the least," whispered Hadley, and we both stifled a giggle—stress does that to you.

"Actually, the opportunity to reschedule an interview is no longer available," Mr. Wells said.

Wait, what? No longer available? I was indignant: "But you said we could!"

"*We?*"

"I mean . . . I. You said I could," I explained.

"Situations change. The only opportunity for the school board to gather is today. . . . So if you cannot accommodate us, I'm afraid to say we cannot accommodate you." Mr. Wells was enjoying this. "Now then, we have several more interviews to conduct but thank you for your consideration."

Mr. Wells was so insanely dismissive! I got the distinct feeling he enjoyed watching Ms. Pitt deflate.

You know in the movie *Dirty Dancing* when Patrick Swayze says, "Nobody puts Baby in the corner"? Well, I was having a similar Momma Bear reaction regarding Ms. Pitt. No one puts Ms. Pitt in the corner! I wasn't about to let her earnest intentions go unnoticed. If this was her one shot at getting the chance to chair the English department, then I was going to make sure she won. I stepped forward to address the board.

"Fine. Then it's go-time. Let's do it now," I said.

"Now? We can't do it NOW!" Hadley said, eyes ablaze with horror.

Mr. Wells looked up, shocked. "I thought you made it clear you weren't up to the task today."

I took a defiant step forward, placed a hand on Ms. Pitt's hip, and I narrowed my (her) eyes. The pose was remotely pro-wrestler macho.

"Bring it," I said calmly.

The board members looked at one another, at once horrified AND confused. "Bring it?" someone mouthed to the person next to her.

"Well . . . she's already here, isn't she?" asked another mouse-ish looking woman.

Mr. Wells responded with ninja calm: "All right, then . . ."

Hadley looked at me with panicked eyes, imploring

me not to go it alone. But it was too late. I knew how badly she wanted this.

And for the first time, I understood how much Ms. Pitt *deserved* it.

I grabbed Hadley's arm and looked into *my* eyes, trying to get through to Ms. Pitt. I whispered, "Now or never. We have to try."

We locked eyes and I felt us connect.

"I won't let you down." We shared a smile and knew that we trusted each other.

"Any day now, Ms. Pitt . . ." Mr. Wells said, exasperated. It was obvious he thought Ms. Pitt was down for the count. "And this is a *private* interview, Hadley. You may step outside." His eyes indicated the door.

Left with no choice, Hadley had to slink out. United in our quest, we spontaneously did a little fist-bump. A few school board members laughed nervously.

Before leaving, Hadley placed the cell phone squarely in my hand. "In case Tatum—" she whispered.

I nodded. Hadley left, and, closing the door behind her, she looked forlorn, like someone being led down a wooden plank. I turned to face the board with all the strength I could muster.

"Now, Ms. Pitt, I'm Carl Papp, school district superintendant. I think we should just jump right in," Carl said, peering over his Coke-bottle glasses.

Maybe it was the stress, I have no idea, but I heard the word *jump* and thought it might break the ice and be hilarious if I jumped into the air. You know, as a general indication that we were "jumping in." I leaped up into the air and knew before my feet planted on the ground that that was an illogical and very stupid thing to do.

"That was . . . 'jumping in,'" I tried to explain.

"I see . . ." Carl said, looking over some papers before him, shaking his head slightly. Mr. Wells was stewing.

"Let me come out and ask the obvious. Why do you want to chair the English department?" asked a heavyset woman with badly frosted hair.

"Oh. That's easy. Because I love love love my students. And when I say love, it's real love, real devotion—not like when some people say, 'Oh, I love Brady Beyersdorf or I love Keith Randle' . . . but deep down you're thinking—yeah, right, but in two months you'll be on to someone else. . . ."

Confused eyes stared back at me. What was their deal? Wasn't my logic convincing? Then I remembered: I needed to sound more like a teacher.

"Seriously, I am *all* about my students. I give everything to them," I explained further.

"Is that a *good* thing?" Mr. Wells asked slyly.

You should know about having no life. You're the one raising pygmy hedgehogs, I wanted to say but bit my tongue. He *so* bugged me.

"I'm just saying . . . I'd do *anything* for my students and that's totally the kind of devotion you want, right? Like, did you know I chair four committees?" I tried to count them in my head and hoped that was the right number.

"Which committees?" asked the pudgy woman.

Oh, crap. Which committees? "Student council. All hail Student Council. . . . Oh, and . . . the Self-Esteem You Rock . . . thingy." I paused, my mind scrambled. I gave up trying to sound like Ms. Pitt. But I didn't give up trying to get her message across. "Look, I was skeptical, too, about the You Rock group, but it's totally cool. . . . Like, during the session or whatever last time, I totally cried. Practically bawling," I said, impressed. I realized they did not seem as impressed. "It was a . . . moment."

"And you consider bawling a . . . good thing?" Mr. Wells inquired. Jeez, all he needed to do now was twirl a mustache and laugh. *Mwah-haw-haw!*

"Yes, I consider it a good thing. Like I said, I try to be real and honest. Which is more than I can say for most teachers," I said.

There was a bit of contrarian buzz on that statement.

"And . . . what other committees do you chair? You

didn't complete your list," asked another board member.

I looked down, my mind firing away. I went through a mental contact list, trying to place where I'd seen Ms. Pitt at school . . . as I visualized her, I realized I *always* saw Ms. Pitt flitting about the school, consummately involved. Some teachers hightailed it out of school as soon as the final bell rang, but not Ms. Pitt. She stuck around and chaired her committees . . . like yearbook—

"Yearbook!" I squealed. "I totally chair yearbook!"

"You '*totally* chair yearbook'?" the heavyset woman echoed.

"Yeah, and Great Books! Great Books, that's it! She asked me to—" I cut myself off before I said the word *join*. Why would I ask myself to join a club I chair? Maybe they didn't catch that. "We discuss great literature that's not just your average *Moby-Dick*." I paused. "Which is not to say anything against *Moby-Dick*—I mean, we wouldn't have the movie *Jaws* without it, for one thing."

Now that I thought about it, Great Books probably *is* a great club to be involved with. But it's not like I have time to read anything other than my required reading. . . . Then again, maybe it was time I did a little bit more than required reading. All I did was study and look where it got me—miserable and switched! I vowed right then and there to myself that if I ever got back, I would take more time to NOT study.

Wait, did I just think that?

"Ms. Pitt. It is obvious you are still not feeling well—" Mr. Wells started.

My face got red. I *had* to prove them wrong.

"Why?" I demanded. "Why do you seem so hell-bent on accusing me of not feeling well?"

"Well . . . your choice of language, for one. Everything is 'totally' this and 'totally' that." Everyone chuckled at his observation.

"So I speak the students' language . . . That's exactly my point! I relate to them and work so freakin' hard for them, you have no idea."

"*Freakin'*?" Carl Papp repeated, uncertain.

"Yes, *freakin'*, and it's about freakin' time you hire someone who not only knows their stuff when it comes to teaching literature, but who also is down with the kids."

"Is *down*?"

What was I, speaking in code? "Understands."

"Right, right . . ."

"All this empathy astounds me. You make it sound like you are quite the saint, Ms. Pitt," Mr. Wells sneered.

"No. I'm no saint. But I *do* give a hundred percent to my kids when it comes to academics, and I also give a hundred percent when it comes to extracurricular. One hundred percent. And you know it and I know it. Maybe I don't always go about it the right way—I'm not perfect—but I try harder than anyone. I'd love for you to prove me wrong, Mr. Wells. Go ahead and please tell the board of another teacher who is more involved with his students than I am," I asked with total conviction.

All board members turned to Mr. Wells, who did not respond. His silence confirmed my devotion, something he could not refute.

Mr. Wells stared down at me. "There's one other thing I'd like to discuss. You seemed rather . . . suspicious of the standardized test prep I was interested in executing."

I *was*? My mind scrambled for a response but it was a big goose egg.

"The tests from the U.S. Department of Education, remember? It's a prep system that has had tremendous results in other regions." He smiled to himself, satisfied. "I was thankful when you finally agreed to administer the sample tests, but it seemed to me that if you were doing such a crackerjack job as a teacher, you wouldn't have resisted such testing so strongly."

And that's when it hit me. In that instant, I totally understood the Mr. Wells/Ms. Pitt clash. Mr. Wells is all about standardized tests, and Ms. Pitt has a more . . . well, a more organic approach. And come to think of it, hadn't I resisted Ms. Pitt for the same reason? Wasn't *I* sort of way too into the standardized tests? Was I a teenage Mr. Wells? More important: *Was raising pygmy hedgehogs in my future?!*

Then I saw the scene between me and Ms. Pitt that had happened in the hallway play in my mind like a flashback in a movie:

Oh, Hadley. To Kill a Mockingbird *is not about vocab words. . . . It's about life. . . .* Ms. Pitt had said.

A smile broke out on my face. Ms. Pitt didn't want me to understand the vocab words, she wanted me to know what the book was truly about! I took a deep breath and chose my words carefully.

"Mr. Wells. I am *all* for academic accountability. Totally. I mean, I agreed to have my students take the sample test, didn't I? It's just that I find it more difficult to test English than, say, math. Because when it comes to understanding literature, there are tons of interpretations. It's not . . . quantifiable like math. Like, take, for example, *Jane Eyre*. It may move me but leave someone else totally cold. Because with literature, as with life, there's often not *one* right answer. That's why I tend to be a bit skeptical of standardized testing. It doesn't tell the full story." I smiled to myself, knowing full well this was coming out *great*. Jeez, even I was impressed with myself. And I could tell by the smiles on the other board members faces, they agreed.

Just then, my cell phone beeped. "Excuse me," I said as I reached for my phone. The caller ID read TATUM. "One sec, just let me read this," I said as I scanned the text.

The board was abuzz—I suppose reading texts mid-interview did look a *bit* flippant.

i need u. scaring myself. meet @ the track.

Tatum's SCARING herself? What did that mean?

It didn't matter. I had to help her. She was my sister and she was in trouble. Period.

"So sorry about this, but I gotta blaze," I said breathlessly.

"Blaze? Now? Exactly where are you going, Ms. Pitt?" Carl Papp inquired.

I took a deep breath. "A student needs me. She's in trouble and she says she's scaring herself. I have to help her." I started for the door and stopped before I exited. "Thank you for the opportunity and just know there's no one that deserves this more than Ms. Pitt. I mean, me." I closed the door behind me.

CHAPTER 13

I opened the car door and jumped into the backseat. "We have to get to the junior high track. Now."

"Wait, what's going on?"

"Tatum texted me. She said she's 'scaring herself,'" I said.

"Oh, dear," Hadley whispered.

Mr. Hudson put the car in motion and we were off. His eyes connected with mine in the rearview mirror. "So? How did the interview go?"

"Good, I think. . . . But then again, it's sorta hard to tell. I mean, I split," I responded. I was relieved the Prius could move so fast; we were sailing toward the junior high track.

"You mean you just—" Hadley said in an agitated tone.

"Took off. Yeah. Tatum's in trouble. THAT'S more important," I said.

Mr. Hudson looked at Hadley as if to suggest, *See my point about Ms. Pitt's devotion?* Then he did a little double-take.

"You know, I must comment. . . . It's nice to see you without your head in a book for once, Hadley. You're always in that library, studying away," Mr. Hudson said. Then his expression changed, as if he were realizing something. "I mean, not that that's a bad thing! It's not. It's great! But . . . there's more to life than studying. Besides, is there really *that* much homework in eighth grade?" he asked.

"I don't know," Hadley responded truthfully. She seemed lost in thought. "You *really* pay attention, don't you, Mr. Hudson?"

"I try. You set the bar pretty high." Mr. Hudson blushed. It was getting a little crowded in the car.

"Can we get back to this little thing called the *interview*?" I asked. "I did all I could do. I sang your praises left and right."

Both Mr. Hudson *and* Hadley whizzed their heads around and gave a quizzical *huh?* Why would I sing Hadley's praises?

"I mean . . . I did the best I could," I explained. "And talked a lot about how devoted *I* am."

Thankfully it didn't take long to get to the junior high. "I'll park the car," Mr. Hudson said. "And I'll see if I can't get the Malibu started again. Hadley, you go find Tatum."

"I'll join you in just a minute," I told Mr. Hudson, and flew out the door, leaving him mystified again.

I could see Tatum in the distance, making lonely loops around the barren junior high track. I should have known we'd find her here. Whenever Tatum was down, she said exercise always made her feel better. It was way more productive than Ben & Jerry's. Tatum had been on the junior high track team and was an incredibly strong runner. She was a natural, like a colt making gloriously strong loops around that course. I marveled at her grace and wondered if my legs would ever look that supple or run that strong. But she'd given up track when she joined high school cheerleading and never looked back. We'd never talked about it, but I'd wondered if doing quasi-ridiculous pony jumps and cheering for boys could ever compare to kicking some serious booty on the track. . . .

"Tatum!" I called. Tatum looked up and saw me—Ms. Pitt—waving wildly.

She looked a bit confused by the sight of Hadley *and* Ms. Pitt, and she tentatively waved back.

"She probably just wants to talk to me," I said. "I did speak to her when she thought I was you and all." I paused long enough to realize that was practically the most insane sentence I'd ever spoken. "But now it's about family. We're really close."

"You're right. I'll go down and talk to her then."

"And no mentioning our switch. Tatum's stressed-out enough," I added. "We'll give you some privacy . . . but maybe I'll just hang out under the bleachers over there."

"What, and eavesdrop?"

"Basically, yeah." I shrugged.

Hadley nodded and headed toward the track. I ducked under the bleachers and watched Tatum and Hadley embrace. Tatum really clung to Hadley, and I felt warm knowing Tatum needed me so badly.

I also managed to hear Tatum and Hadley's entire exchange—score!

"Oh, Hadley . . ." Tatum said, her cheeks wet with tears. "Did Ms. Pitt tell you?" She looked at Hadley with red eyes and a snotty nose and she *still* was vaguely glamorous. The nerve! Who does that?

"She did—she was worried about you. And I'm so sorry, Tatum," Hadley said. "So sorry."

"I'm pathetic. This whole thing is so embarrassing. I

applied to a lot of schools. I mean, a *lot* of schools. Not even the greatest or the most competitive of schools! And you know how many of them wanted me? Zero. None. Nada. Zilch," she said, and with each descriptive term for goose egg, she got more and more upset.

Hadley hugged her again. Tatum was so special and probably thought the world had taken a cruel turn and would continue on this horrid course forever.

"I mean, I applied to schools I thought were, you know, below me or something. Guess I shouldn't have been so snotty, huh?" She blew her nose on her sleeve. "My life is over. What am I gonna do?" Tatum started to really cry again.

Hadley took a deep breath, grabbed Tatum, and looked her dead in the eye. "I tell you what you're going to do. You're going to deal with it and everything is going to be absolutely fine."

Tatum was taken aback with Hadley's strong turn. "It is?"

"Absolutely. Because you know what can be the best thing for your soul sometimes?" Hadley asked with a sage twinkle in her eye.

"No. What?"

"*Not getting what you want.* Sometimes not getting

125

what you want is *exactly* what you need."

"What do you mean?" Tatum was skeptical.

"Because when you don't get what you want, that's precisely when you learn the most."

"I've learned I may be the most popular loser in town."

"All right, no more talk like that. Period. You know deep down you're an exceptional person, Tatum. You're kind and you're creative and you have gifts. You may not have gotten into your first choice of college—"

"Or the eighteenth," Tatum interrupted.

"Or the eighteenth, sure. But life is NOT over. You can easily get into a community college, work hard, and transfer to a great state school. People do that all the time," Hadley explained.

Tatum looked down, forlorn. "You mean a lamebrain state school."

Hadley took a deep breath. "Listen to me. Could you handle turning out like Woody Allen or Jonas Salk?"

"Sure . . ."

"Well, they're both state school grads and they seem to have done okay in life. Ever heard of Ball State University?" Hadley asked.

"*Ball State?* Ick. Where's that?"

"Muncie, Indiana. And it was good enough for David Letterman. He has a hall there that's dedicated to all the C students of the world," Hadley went on.

"He does?" Tatum's eyes grew larger—she was feeling better, it was obvious.

"Yup. Bottom line, Tatum, is that it's not *where* you get your education, but *what* you do with it. It's not your popularity or hair or boyfriend, it's *you* that matters."

"Jeez, Hadley. How'd you get so smart? You are such the Jedi brilliant little sister. Seriously, you're like my personal Yoda, aren't you?" Tatum joked. She then broke into her excellent Yoda impersonation. "Such wisdom are you. Much brainpower in young package . . ."

Hadley had to laugh. "So you're feeling better?"

Tatum nodded. "Look, I'm still a little screwed. But . . . I could handle turning out like David Letterman. I'd be fine with that," Tatum said.

"Yeah, you'd be okay with your own TV show? That could work?" Hadley joked.

"Yeah, I could deal with that just fine."

"So you're sure you're going to be all right, then?" Hadley looked into Tatum's green pools that had some of their trademark sparkle back.

"Eventually." Tatum grinned.

They hugged, and I knew I had to hightail it back to the car before Tatum was clued into the fact that I had basically spied on their entire exchange. I didn't want to be downgraded from diligent, involved teacher to obsessive creep in one fell swoop!

CHAPTER 14

When I got to the parking lot, I turned to wait for Hadley.

And I gotta say—usually you never get to see yourself except on the occasional family video or some random filming of a piano recital, which inevitably is a wooden, false representation of what you really look like. I studied myself and wondered if Ms. Pitt made *my* body move differently or if that was *really* what I looked like. Did I stand like that? Walk like that? It was almost like when you get into those really bizarre moods and stare at your reflection, almost asking out loud, like in a bad after-school special, *Who am I? Who am I* really? Is that . . . me? Well, I got to do that through another myopic and potentially warped lens. I realized Hadley—I—wasn't nearly as tragic-looking as maybe I had feared. Sure, I was no Tatum—frankly, who was? Overall, the effect wasn't disastrous. I had to bottle this revelation.

"Did I hear right? Is she okay?" I asked breathlessly.

"Tatum is going to be fine. She's going to investigate some community colleges now and it doesn't seem as bleak," Hadley said with a grin.

"Oh, thank goodness. I'm so relieved. Thank you. Because if anyone is unequipped to deal with things going wrong, it's Tatum. I mean—the streetlights see her coming and they practically turn green on cue," I said.

"Oh, I wouldn't be so sure," Hadley responded. "Maybe that's what *you* see, but I doubt Tatum feels that. You may think Tatum has everything, but maybe today has taught you that no one's perfect."

"Maybe there's just perfect students. Like 4.9 GPA–Cindy Pang, for instance."

Hadley shook her head. "Again . . . no one is perfect. No one." She paused and studied me. "You really need to figure that one out, don't you?"

I was stunned.

"In fact, *perfectionism is slow death*," Hadley said slowly with Ms. Pitt's distinct earth mother delivery.

"Who said that?" I asked.

"Someone very, very smart."

I looked down at the ground and realized tears were kinda sorta welling in my eyes. Okay, today *was* an emotional day and I was potentially losing my mind, but what

Ms. Pitt said rang true. I have been knocking myself out and slaving over homework and obsessing over being perfect at school because I feel so inadequate compared to my sister's perfection. But perhaps Ms. Pitt was right—there ain't no such thing.

And then Ms. Pitt's wisdom boomeranged right back to me! She wasn't so innocent on this one, either. "Sounds like you could learn a lot from yourself," I said.

"How's that?"

"You're telling me not to obsess about perfection, blah blah blah—"

"*Blah blah blah?*"

"Hear me out," I said. "You *yourself* are guilty of trying to be this perfect teacher. You know—the most prepared, the most involved, the most beloved. . . . blah blah blah . . ." I savored the words. "And, as they say, '*perfection is a slow death.*'"

Hadley grinned at me as the thought took form, and I could tell it was resonating. "Okay . . . you're an honor student for a reason. And it's *not* just because you study entirely too much."

"Let's hope you still feel that way even if the school board totally boots your butt to the curb," I joked.

"With Mr. Wells, anything is possible. . . ." Hadley said.

"Including . . . slow dancing with him tonight?" I said, at once laughing and gagging over the thought.

"Slow dance with Mr. Wells? Are you pathologically *insane*?" Hadley asked.

"But there's the I-Hate-Mondays Dance tonight, remember? Look, before I wouldn't have given a rip, either, but you gotta go—*Zane specifically asked if I'd be there*! Do you know what that means to me?" I asked, and I think I was actually vibrating.

"I have some idea," Hadley said. "It's somewhere on the scale in between needing oxygen and electricity."

"Because maybe . . . just maybe . . . Zane *did* send me that Secret Admirer Candy-Gram. And maybe . . . just maybe . . . he *is* interested in me and not just in my sister," I said with near-pride in my voice. I'm not sure I believed it but I could try.

"Okay. I'll do it. For you, I'll do it," Hadley said. "But I really think we should focus on this teeny-tiny obstacle called *switching us back*."

"Yeah . . . Maybe we should head on down and enroll at the Switch Our Bodies Back School." I paused and realized maybe that sounded a bit harsh. But my nerves were frayed.

We both jumped when Mr. Hudson drove up in his sad old Chevy and honked the horn. "Lucky I carry jumper cables." He leaned out of his car window, seeming a little uncertain of his role. That made two of us. . . .

"Excuse me . . . ladies," Mr. Hudson fumbled. "Just wondering if everything's okay."

"Yeah, yeah," I responded. "It's cool."

He nodded. "And Tatum is . . ."

"Fine. She's fine now," Hadley said.

"Terrific. Well done, Hadley. Then . . . might I suggest I take everyone home? You, too, Carol. It's been a long day and you look like you could use a chauffeur."

Aw! Mr. Hudson was so cute! I hoped the object of his affection was picking up on it.

"That's very kind of you, *Randy*," I said meaningfully. Did the top of his ears turn pink?

"Plus, I have to prepare for tomorrow's class now if I'm going to go to that dance tonight," Mr. Hudson said.

"Right. That terrifically important dance," Hadley said. And I think she meant it.

CHAPTER 15

Hadley climbed out of the car when we drove up to her house. *My* house.

On her way out, she whispered to me, "So . . . the family will be home now, yes?"

I guess she had reason to be nervous about walking into a house she'd barely ever been to before. At least I knew Ms. Pitt lived alone. The worst that could happen when I walked into her place would be her cats would use their feline senses and freak out because I wasn't truly their owner and maybe attack with a giant hairball.

"Mom should be home at least. She's probably back from ceramics."

"Are you some kind of mind reader? How do you know all this stuff?" Mr. Hudson asked incredulously.

"Oh . . . Mo—I mean, *Mrs. Fox* was, uh, in a class of mine. A ceramics class, that is. She made a duck," I stammered. "I made a bowl." Mr. Hudson nodded as if this made some sort of sense.

"See you tonight," Hadley said.

"See you tonight," I joined, and again, we did our little fist-bump. With that, Hadley walked slowly up the path, almost as if she were approaching a haunted house. On some level, that made sense. . . . Maybe we were ghosts? Something supernatural *had* to be afoot.

Mr. Hudson pulled away. "And you live on Virginia Drive, don't you, Carol?" he asked.

"Sounds good." I smiled back at him. "And thanks for being a chauffeur today. Totally cool of you."

"My pleasure." We drove in pleasant silence and he pulled onto Virginia Drive. He scanned the houses and looked to me for confirmation. Like I knew which one was Ms. Pitt's house? "Here you go," he said, pulling up to a house. "Your blue bungalow. It is cozy, just as you described." At least somebody knew where to go. . . .

"Right. Cool. Well, thanks again," I said, and tore out of the car, fumbling through Ms. Pitt's purse for her keys. I could sense Mr. Hudson wanted some final connection but that was waaaay out of the question for my thirteen-year-old self! I had never even kissed a boy before, and my first kiss sure wasn't going to be with some forty-year-old man—how gross can you get?!

"I'll see you tonight, Carol. You will be there?" he

called out the window. I didn't respond immediately and Mr. Hudson looked a bit worried. "At the dance, I mean?"

"I'll be there, Mr. Hudson," I said. I mean, I had to see if Zane was into *me* . . . if I ever got back to being me, that is!

His eyes warmed again. "All right. And it's Randy, remember? So I'll see you then. Hey, and if you need a ride tonight—"

"That's cool. I'm good. Thanks," I said over my shoulder. "See you there. Bye!" I went up to the cozy blue bungalow and wondered if this was truly Ms. Pitt's house. Why hadn't I asked her for the address? My mind wasn't working. . . . I tried to put a key in the door. It didn't fit. So I tried another key. Nothing.

Mr. Hudson hadn't budged. He was smiling but seemed a bit suspicious, watching me fumble with the keys. How long could I keep this charade up? It was exhausting!

I noticed another blue bungalow across the street. In fact, there were some smallish, funky sculptures in the front lawn that screamed Ms. Pitt. She would have those wind chimes up, all right, and they'd be tinkling in the wind. I crossed the street and said on the way to an increasingly befuddled Mr. Hudson, "Just kidding!" He smiled again.

I knew intuitively this was her house. And, like the shoe fitting Cinderella's foot, the key slid into place. At last! I gave one final wave and Mr. Hudson tooted his horn and drove off. Man oh man, does that guy have it bad for me. Or Ms. Pitt. You know what I mean. . . .

I turned on a light and I know it sounds like the most fundamentally "duh" realization, but I was amazed Ms. Pitt had a house. Or more specifically, that she had a life separate from school at all! Didn't she just pull out a cot or something from behind her desk and camp out at school? Where did teachers go at night? Did they have normal lives or did they lead a life of secrets? Did they get Netflix and maybe—just maybe—furtively love slasher movies? Did they drink wine? Did they argue with their husbands? Did they like being a teacher?

I took a step into Ms. Pitt's pleasant little house and soaked up her environs. I never before would have told you that purple walls work, but Ms. Pitt had selected a soft mauvey tone that soothed. The artwork that plastered the walls was decidedly amateurish but still charming somehow. A beautiful gray cat meowed and jumped off the couch to greet me. "Hey, girl . . . or guy . . . hey, cat," I said, and bent down to pet the kitty.

But the cat stopped midtracks and gave a serious scowl. He yowled and hissed, turned around and trotted off. Darn those intuitive cats—that's why I preferred simple, sloppy dogs. A golden retriever would have zero clue to our mistaken identity and come bounding up, I was positive. I've said it once and I'll say it again: You don't see cats leading the blind.

"Hiss to you, too, then," I said to the cat who cowered in the corner. "We'll see if I feed *you* in the morning." Then I wondered about tomorrow morning. Oh, dear, would I wake up in Ms. Pitt's body?! Not another day of this. . . . Somehow we *had* to get switched back!

Soaking in Ms. Pitt's environment temporarily distracted me. I intently studied the zillion framed pictures on the walls, including some choice shots of Ms. Pitt when she was a little girl—it was so clearly her same cherubic face. She was truly adorable with scruffy ponytails and a somewhat serious pout. There was a definite trace of sadness in the pictures, though, and I found my heart hurt a bit thinking about what she had said about her own upbringing and her parents' lack of interest in her.

I was amazed to see a shot of a twentysomething Ms. Pitt on the slopes at Vail, looking like a veritable ski bunny. Who knew? In one picture, she was surrounded by friends, all of whom looked like they biked to work and drank nothing but green healthy goo. They were on the beach, all smiling, all suntanned. It looked like Ms.

Pitt was the lone single person in a sea of couples. *That must be hard*, I thought, and I recognized that same low-grade sadness even in the shots where her smile was big. It was always sort of there with Ms. Pitt, like a little rain cloud.

A frame was decorated with little apples and read SCHOOL DAYS across the top. In the picture, Ms. Pitt looked to be about thirteen years old—probably exactly the age I am now—and she had a small, shy smile on her lips. But in this shot, she didn't look sad; she looked like her soul was softly singing. She had her arm around another woman, probably her teacher. The teacher was clutching her strongly and you felt the pride in this woman's embrace, her Momma Bear protectiveness.

Underneath the photo it read: MISS MULLIGAN & ME.

I inched closer toward the photo, studying all the details. Ms. Pitt was rather average looking and a bit awkward but you felt her spirit soaring and a smile aching to be fully released. I could sense that with Miss Mulligan's encouragement, Ms. Pitt had felt important for the first time.

I just want to be a Miss Mulligan for someone else.

I heard Ms. Pitt's words reverberate in my brain and instantly I felt terrible. I knew how badly she wanted to chair the English department, how much she wanted to be like Miss Mulligan and help others. And I felt a thunderous ache that I had most likely let her down. Granted, what did I know about being a teacher or chairing an English department? But by leaving midway through the interview itself and being focused on Tatum and myself and not on Ms. Pitt's interests . . . well, I had probably dropped the ball.

Big-time.

Then again, I had really tried to defend her and get her the position, but leaving could not have sent a good message to the school board. I felt terrible.

I wandered around her house, inspecting every nook and cranny. Her fridge was predictably stocked with organic this and tofu that and I wondered how she subsisted on that stuff. Yuck. Surely she must crave some Red Vines or Dr Pepper or something occasionally! Besides, isn't sugar from sugar cane a natural source? I consider sugar a health food.

Her closet was as unsurprising as her refrigerator. There was a heap of peasant skirts and various tops—linens and organic wraps. Her shoes were all sensible and I said aloud, "Hello, Grandma." It's not as if I teeter around all day on high heels, but these shoes were ridiculous. She was in her mid-thirties, not mid-sixties!

I mean, if the retro Volkswagen Beetle was a wardrobe,

this would be it: small and sparse, vaguely hippie and comfortable, no-nonsense. It killed me, because Ms. Pitt truly was an attractive woman but she looked like she barely gave a second thought to her clothes or bothered with her hair. She didn't show off—or even just accentuate—her slim figure. She kept herself hidden under mountains and layers of fabric. She wasn't buttoned up, she was drowning.

In Ms. Pitt's office was a treasure trove. She had stacks and stacks of papers and books, mostly on the topic of teaching (also, her literature collection was thorough, I will say, which was no surprise). And everything was well-worn and obviously had been read—she had everything from classics to modern fiction to history and beyond, absolutely everything under the sun. There were also such titles as *Teach Like Your Hair's on Fire* and *Teaching Outside the Box: How to Grab Your Students by Their Brains* and *Teaching to Change Lives: 7 Proven Ways to Make Your Teaching Come Alive*. And that was just the first stack.

More shocking was all the school paperwork. Many, many trees died for this cause. (Come to think of it, how could a staunch environmentalist like Ms. Pitt agree to be a teacher? They were the biggest wasters of paper of all! Then I remembered Ms. Pitt said she would only use recycled paper—I had completely forgotten she had started that trend at Burroughs Junior High.)

I just couldn't believe all the files and papers. And I suppose it all had to be graded! I couldn't imagine how much time that would take.

Ms. Pitt even had an "idea corkboard" that was littered with random thoughts about how to teach, inspiring quotes, and pictures. At the center of the idea corkboard was another picture of Miss Mulligan. I got the distinct feeling Miss Mulligan was at the center of much of Ms. Pitt's personal philosophy. . . .

Out of the corner of my eye, I spotted a "Student of the Year" folder! Being a Student of the Year was this big deal and whoever won that title got to come on the stage before a packed school auditorium and have their praises sung by teachers, faculty, and fellow students. It was the stuff of junior high legend, and the title would obviously be great to someday put on a transcript to Stanford. . . .

I snagged it greedily and tore it open. Of course there was a recommendation for Cindy Pang, the academic virtuoso. Cindy must have come out of the womb knowing fractions and being able to spell "extraordinary." Which was what she was. She was also most likely going to any college of her choice.

I flipped another paper and was shocked to see *my name*!

HADLEY FOX.

I couldn't believe it! Had Ms. Pitt actually recommended *me*?!

My eyes tore over the page, drinking it in. I felt my pulse race and my throat got dry. I felt so voyeuristic and remotely evil. . . . I knew I shouldn't be reading this but it was impossible to stop, like finding a friend's diary carelessly left open. What are you supposed to do, look away? As if!

Hadley Fox is a delight. She is one of those rare students who takes her academics and thoughts seriously. She will do whatever it takes to not only get it right, but to make right better.

I beamed to myself on that one and felt my self-esteem swell. Maybe Ms. Pitt WAS paying attention! Maybe she DID know her stuff! Why couldn't I see it before? She was clearly seeing me! I read on.

Hadley works as hard as any student I've ever come in contact with in my nine years of teaching, but—

My heart froze. "But" was *never* good.

—but Hadley needs to broaden her scope if she is to truly blossom. Hadley is by far my best student. She is always prepared and under her cool exterior, she's tremendously sensitive and thoughtful. Yet I wish I got to see MORE of Hadley. Not just the straight-A student,

but Hadley the human being. She seems resistant to let anyone in. Even her friends are not as important to her as her grades.

I stopped reading and let this thump around in my heart. Its truth seared me and it stung. It stung bad. I kept reading:

I realized in filling out this application for Student of the Year I write easily about Hadley's academic achievements but knew little about who she was. She is not the most well-rounded. To succeed in life, one must achieve a balance, and Hadley Fox, I am forced to report, is sorely lacking on that front.

I cannot recommend Hadley at this time.

My heart skipped a beat.

I cannot recommend Hadley . . .

Bye-bye.

I sat down on Ms. Pitt's floor and began to softly cry.

CHAPTER 16

I had barely managed to stray from my sad heap on the floor. I'm not sure how long I sat there as waves of sadness and pity kept crashing onto me. Here I was, this compulsive studier, the consummate 4.3 student, but for what? To be a shell of a person who isn't well-rounded enough to be Student of the Year and who *still* forgets about preparing for oral presentations?

On top of it, I was still switched with Ms. Pitt and that alone was cause for serious pause. How long could this go on? Maybe this was some sort of punishment for my prior nonlife, wasting my teenage years with one solitary goal: Academic success. Whatever that meant.

My thoughts were interrupted by a phone that kept ringing and ringing. I ignored it, but the person on the other end of the line sure was a persistent bugger: They kept calling back over and over. And then I remembered: Maybe it was Ms. Pitt—I mean, *me*—calling to check in. Maybe she wanted to coordinate with me as I had been insistent on attending tonight's dance. But that was before I realized my whole entire life was a colossal joke and I was impossible to nominate as Student of the Year.

Now even the dance seemed like an empty exercise.

On what was practically the nineteenth ring, I reached for the phone. Make that *reluctantly* reached for the phone.

"Hello?" I said glumly, hoping to broadcast my general malaise.

"What's going on, Hadley? Are you okay? Why haven't you been answering the phone?" It was my own voice on the phone. "I've been trying and trying to get through—"

"Yeah, yeah, yeah. Let's cut with the 'I'm so concerned' charade, all right?" I interrupted.

There was a pause. "What's going on?"

I thought about not getting into it but realized, What do I have to lose? Everything seemed lost, anyway. "I found your Student of the Year file. I read everything." I paused for effect. "Hadley Fox . . . *cannot recommend.*"

"Oh, boy. Hadley, you should not have read that. You know I *wanted* to recommend you. And it was easy to write about all your shining talents—"

"*But*—" I interjected for her.

"But . . . I stand by what I wrote. It's true. Was true. I just didn't have a sense of who you were as a person. But that was before today. And today has been . . . illuminating."

I sparked a bit. "Illuminating, huh?" I prayed that didn't sound too hopeful.

"Yes. You've shown me who you *really* are today, Hadley. And I never would have known the real you before. But after I saw you with your sister and your concern for her, and frankly, how you've handled this entirely too nutty body-switching debacle . . . well, now I may just rewrite that last paragraph," Hadley said.

"Really?"

"Really."

I smiled to myself and felt my fog lift. "Thanks. It means a lot."

"My pleasure. I'd actually already thought about it before you'd said a thing."

"So I gotta know," I said, eager to move on. (Emotion is sometimes not my strong suit, and today I was a positively way-too-weepy emo-teen or something.) "How's it going at home?"

"Well . . . your mom and I have bonded over our love of the Carpenters."

"Who?" I was clueless. *The Carpenters?* Were we

having work done on our house or something?

Hadley laughed. "The Carpenters was a band from the seventies—you know, the Paleolithic era. My parents played their albums all the time. Your mom was a little shocked I could sing all of "On Top of the World" with her, to say the least."

"So . . . is the jig up, then? Did Mom figure it out?" I was panicking slightly.

"She thought something was off but she didn't jump to the my-daughter-switched-places-with-her-teacher conclusion."

"Probably not."

"And Tatum did my hair and makeup. There's some serious flowy hair goin' on over here. . . ."

"Yeah . . . Tatum lives for that sorta stuff. Say the word *makeover* and her eyes dilate."

I heard a laugh on the other end of the line. "Regardless, she did a darn fine job. . . . she's good. I—I mean, *you*—look amazing."

I jolted upright. "I do?!"

"What's the term . . . *smokin'*? Yeah, you look smokin'."

A huge smile broke out on my face. *Smokin'* is definitely one term I have *never* heard myself referred to as. And I liked it, I gotta admit. I *am* a girl, after all!

"But not smokin' as in actual cigarettes, you know, smokin' as in—"

"Smokin' hot." I laughed. "I know what you meant."

"Exactly. Zane won't know what hit him," she said, and I practically squealed. That's right—the dance! Tonight! "Are you ready?"

I looked down at Ms. Pitt's dorky attire and dreadfully undone hair. Which was just the start of her problems. I also knew that inside her closet there wasn't exactly a wealth of fashion-forward options.

"Not exactly . . ."

"Well, hop to it! Randy awaits!"

Randy? Oh, Mr. Hudson. Okay, it seemed like there were other priorities to focus on besides looking fetching for a substitute teacher with sad taste in neckwear.

"But Ms. Pitt—" I started.

"And I know what you're thinking," she said. "Why bother with looking cute when we, you know, haven't even switched back yet."

"The thought had crossed my mind."

"Well, this may be going out on a limb, but it seems that our chances of getting unswitched are more likely if we're in the same location," she said. And I had to hand it to her, the point made sense. "Besides. Don't you want to see Zane at the dance?"

My attention perked up. I did, actually. Especially if I was looking smokin'—that I wanted to see! And maybe any newfound hotness could potentially offset the strangeness of having Ms. Pitt speak for me. "Yeah. I am curious."

"Me, too. Meet you there in an hour, renominated Student of the Year." I had to grin to myself. "And *no* driving."

I let out a little defeated protest sigh. I thought she'd forgotten. "Awww . . ."

"No driving. You can walk or bike, I really don't care, but no driving. I need you in one piece. See you soon."

Tatum sure had a point about Ms. Pitt. She *was* the best.

CHAPTER 17

Back in the depths of Ms. Pitt's closet, I found a lone pair of stunning heels, practically unworn and still tucked away in their original box. There must have been some special occasion where Ms. Pitt busted out the swanky heels. It was about time Ms. Pitt put something on that said, "Over here!" and not, "Look the other way!"

I slid into the shoes and took a look in a full-length mirror. I pivoted to the side, just as I'd seen women do in all the movies, inspecting the overall effect. And as I'm not exactly the most savvy on a pair of heels, I tee-tered over and collapsed onto a nearby bed. I laughed to myself and got back in the saddle, as they say, and pulled myself up. I practiced walking around the room, cautiously planting the heels one foot after another. I felt like Bambi taking his wobbly first steps . . . and with each step, I gained more confidence. Soon heels didn't feel *as* foreign. Very cool!

Now it was time to find something a bit more alluring. Nothing linen, nothing shapeless, and nothing organic, *please*. I'm all for the environment, but does every evening have to be green-friendly? Besides . . . silk comes from silkworms, doesn't it? Is there a rule that organic has to be dowdy? I was going to step it up for Ms. Pitt and show off her inner babe.

I found a lovely wrap dress that would play up Ms. Pitt's shape. I had no idea why I'd never seen her in this before. . . . It was flattering and sexy without being in your face. Because I really hate that over-the-top sexpot thing.

Oh, how I wished I had Tatum on hand to help craft the hair and makeup. For one, Ms. Pitt had a limited selection of products. For two, I pretty much had limited to zero idea what I was doing. Still, I carried on and tried to assemble her hair in a more manageable style. Heck, I was trying to give her a style, period! Her hair was luxurious and she had mounds of it—unlike my sad head of straw—but I didn't know what to do with it. It was a monster unto itself. I tried an updo, which was disastrous. I tried a half updo, which was disastrous. I let it hang down, which was disastrous. (There seemed to be a theme here.) So I grabbed one of those mammoth hair clamps I always see girls wearing—you know, they look sort of like the Jaws of Life or something—and threw her hair into an updo and clamped down. Miraculously, it stayed put! And more miraculously, it was pretty! It was sloppy-fabulous and I was pleased. With a spot of lip gloss and some under-eye concealer (seriously, there was some darkness going on there), Ms. Pitt looked smashing. One glance of this glammed-up Ms. Pitt, and Mr. Hudson would most likely spontaneously combust.

I decided I was feeling so darling and vaguely European (if that's possible in San Marino, California) that I decided to ride a bike to the dance, too. It seemed like a Parisian solution somehow and made sense.

With the wind in my face, I pedaled toward the school. The early evening was just warm enough and I felt oddly happy. Then I remembered I was trapped in my teacher's body and the sense of elation crashed. But . . . I pedaled a *bit* more maniacally when I realized Zane would be at the dance. And there still was the debate as to who exactly sent me that Candy-Gram. . . .

CHAPTER 18

I zigzagged through a throng of students littering the walkway into school. I had to hand it to the Student Council and perhaps even begrudgingly praise Kaya Tisch (trust me—*that's* never happened before). Apparently this I-Hate-Mondays Dance idea was a hit. There was a palpable energy coursing through the air.

I paid my two-dollar entrance fee and received a hand stamp—as if this was some sort of wild club or something. As I entered the cafeteria, I was amazed by the transformed space—was this actually the spot where we ate that objectionable food and gossiped? There were twinkly lights everywhere and it was vaguely pretty and romantic. Students were everywhere and I stood back for a moment to take it all in. But my moment was ruined as I was accosted by Nan and Soup.

"Ms. Pitt, have you seen Hadley?" Soup asked desperately.

You have no idea how badly I wanted to grab his shoulders and say, *It's me, idiot! Your best friend! Hadley!*

This whole situation was so utterly improbable. Seriously, you should try having your best friends ask if they've seen you when you're trapped in your English teacher's body—it's a mind-scrambler. Before I could respond, I saw both Soup's and Nan's faces change. Their scrunched-up look of general confusion and concern were replaced by delight. At least I think that was it.

"Whoa, Ms. Pitt, you look amazing. Snap!" Nan said breathlessly. She seemed genuinely stunned.

I smiled. "I do, don't I?" I twirled a bit but soon realized this sounded highly arrogant—obviously I wasn't talking about *myself*! "I mean, I really should try to clean up now and again."

"Well, keep it up," Nan half joked. "Anyway, have you seen Hadley? We've been looking all over for her and you know she was a total freak earlier today."

"Yeah, she's like totally unreachable and is nowhere to be found," said Soup. "Which is so not like her. We have no idea what the bleep is going on."

"Yeah, well, that makes bleepin' all of us," I said.

Nan and Soup looked shocked and laughed a bit. "Anyway, if you see her, Ms. Pitt, let her know we're looking for her. I mean, you saw how insane she was after this morning," Nan said.

"Yeah. Certifiable," I noted drily.

"I swear, one tanked oral report and it's like the end of the world for Hadley," Soup said. "What she doesn't get is she'd still be awesome if she got nothing but C's."

I felt a big lump in my throat. There's nothing like hearing something unexpectedly kind about yourself. "Awww, Soup. That is so sweet."

Soup shrugged his shoulders, a bit weirded out. "See ya," he said as he and Nan walked away, whispering conspiratorially. I'm sure he thought Ms. Pitt was officially insane.

I shook my head in disbelief over the continued strangeness and scanned the dance, hoping to find myself (trust me, try to avoid this). Instead, I found Zane standing nearby, and at the sight of him, I let out a strange little teenage gurgle.

Ooops.

Zane did not need Ms. Pitt totally vibing on him. I tried to act a bit more teacher, which is way hard when you're dealing with mega-under-the-radar-hotties like Zane Henderson.

"Hello, Zane," I said a bit officiously. "I'm so psyched you and Hadley could team up today."

"Yeah . . . but, uh . . . I actually should be the one

thanking you," he responded.

"*Really?!*"

Just at that moment, I finally spotted Hadley from across the gym. And if I do say so, I clean up well, too! Tatum must have gone to town and the effect was amazing! I looked so—dare I say it?—nice . . . no, better than nice! I mean, I had an actual hairdo, for one, and my hair had some loose waves. There was obvious effort involved but it wasn't over the top. I just looked softer and more beguiling. Pretty, even. And were those kitten heels?

"Whoa," Zane said softly. I realized he had seen me, too! And it caused a "whoa"! Do you have any idea what that does to a girl like me? Any idea at all?

Zane stared at Hadley in the distance and his appreciation was painfully apparent. He looked positively moony—that's a word, right, moony?—as he watched me get confronted by Soup and Nan. It was obvious this interrogation was full tilt. "It just stinks she's dating Soup," he said.

"*What?!*" I squealed like an overly caffeinated teenager. I couldn't help myself!

Me? Dating Soup?!

My emotional overshare instantly got Zane incredibly self-conscious. But he had to get the 4-1-1 on the non-dating status of me and Soup. "Okay, Zane, you have got to trust me on this one, okay? There is *no* way Hadley is dating Soup. As if!"

"No?"

"No! Never! They are *so* not together! They're just friends! Seriously!"

"Well . . ." Zane was uncertain about this enthusiasm from his teacher, and I had to dial it back. Pronto. But that may just be a little bit impossible based on *the fact Zane Henderson may like me, Hadley Della Fox*!!!

Wait. He liked me when I was Hadley Della Fox, who was actually in Hadley's body . . . now I'm this mumbo-jumbo mixed-up mess!

I tried to restrain my enthusiasm and broadcast teacher. I cleared my throat and dropped my voice, sounding more formal. "That's curious, Zane. . . ." Okay, that voice drop was a *bit* too much. "Because I thought perhaps you had a thing for Hadley's sister, Tatum Fox."

"Why would you think that?" Zane asked. His green eyes glowed and he smelled good—all soapy goodness. He wasn't one of these smelly stinky teenage boy monsters who rarely showered.

"Oh . . . uh . . . I jumped to conclusions, I suppose. Aren't all boys in love with Tatum?"

"I'm sure a lot of guys are, sure. Tatum's beautiful."

Of course. My heart sank.

"But so is Hadley. And I've always liked her looks better. Plus Hadley's so smart. Maybe it has to do with the fact that my mom's a professor. I guess I've always had a thing for smarties," Zane explained.

God bless your brilliant mother! I thought. It was all I could do not to kiss him. Ewww. Come to think of it, teacher kissing student = not the best idea. Scratch that.

"Well, Zane, I cannot express to you enough how exciting I think that bit of information is." I smiled, trying to dampen my beam. Really, Ms. Pitt shouldn't be that over the moon hearing about an eighth-grade crush.

Finally, I caught Hadley's eye from across the dance floor and gave a sly little thumbs-up to indicate things were developing with Zane. I was fairly certain she saw me, but Soup and Nan had Hadley cornered.

"So you're really sure about Soup and Hadley not being together?" Zane asked, still mesmerized by—and I love this sentence—*me*!

"Positive. They've been friends and friends only for years. It's more of a brother and sister thing, I swear," I gushed.

"You know what's up with everyone, don't you, Ms. Pitt?"

"You have no idea." I smiled and looked deep into his green pools. "And truth be told, I have a feeling Hadley has a bit of a crush on you."

"Seriously?" His eyes lit up!

"Oh, I'm pretty serious," I said, and I practically had to bite my cheek.

"Thanks, Ms. Pitt."

"Oh no. *Thank you*, Zane." Oh, how I loved saying his name! Zane! Zane! Zane!

"I'm gonna go over there and talk to her, then," he said as if psyching himself up. Who would have thought Zane Henderson needed encouragement?

"I think that's a terrific idea," I said as Zane started to turn. "Oh, and Zane—"

"Yeah?"

"Hadley's had a freaky day. Just keep that in mind if she seems a little . . . weird or something."

"Will do." And with that, I watched him saunter across the dance floor, headed straight for Hadley, Soup, and Nan. I followed at a discreet distance.

Nan saw him approaching, too. "Okay, Zane is so walking over here. . . ." she stage-whispered with a definite thrill in her voice. "Totally walking over here . . . totally walking over here . . ." Nan kept repeating in an excited murmur. Hadley practically clocked Nan in the arm trying to silence her.

Zane stopped in front of Hadley.

And then my general delight crashed. Wait a second! Sure, it's fabulous I now know that Zane likes me, but this isn't how it's supposed to go. At all!

Because there is Zane—the love of my life, the most underestimated and just-under-the-radar sexy thirteen-year-old male to ever grace the planet—and he is stopping to talk to ME at a dance! A dance where they are going to soon play a predictable, drippy slow song that could potentially lead him to actually request the favor of my presence on the dance floor! Which means basically I'd get to HUG him for four minutes, and, P.S., that sounds absolutely nauseating and fabulous. But on this most phenomenal day in which romance is possible for the first time of my life, I am in my teacher's body!

Seriously, who else would this happen to except me?

I willed Ms. Pitt to please please for the love of humanity please be cool and please do not botch my potential love life. Because when we got our bodies back (and that was a really big if, I realized), I would like to have an actual future with Zane Henderson.

Can she see *me* shooting daggers from *her* eyes into *my* body and *her* soul?

Daggers weren't enough. I couldn't let this monumental exchange just happen. . . . I had to be there, hear it, do something. I had to be ready to interject if need be.

I sneaked around a group of students and hid behind a decidedly faux-looking faux palm tree, craning with all my might to hear everything.

"Hi," Zane said to Hadley.

Nan and Soup clearly must have sensed the magnitude of this moment as I watched them sneak off, gesturing behind Zane's back that this was tremendously cool. Hadley swiped at them, indicating they should just move it along.

"Hello," Hadley responded. "So. Can you believe this is where we eat lunch?" She gestured to the twinkling lights. "The lights are so . . . twinkly."

I slapped my hand onto my head. *Twinkly?*

"Yeah. Pretty cool," Zane said. He smiled awkwardly and looked down as an upbeat dance number wound down. And you know what that meant . . .

The distinct opening sounds of Plain White T's "Hey There Delilah" filled the cafeteria and I saw Zane instantly get more red in the face.

"Good song," Zane said.

"Yeah—"

"Wannadance?" he spat out.

Hadley peered over Zane's shoulder to see me practically falling over the palm tree, trying to overhear this action. Hadley shot me a look. "All right, why not?"

Hadley answered, obviously wanting to get Zane away from me, the fumbling weirdo.

Couples filled the dance floor and a surrounding crowd of envious onlookers watched from the outer rim of the cafeteria. Zane and Hadley were square in the center of the couples and I just had to make sure there'd be enough distance between them.

I crept closer, awkwardly circling the dancing students. I must have looked positively psychotic, edging closer and closer to Zane and Hadley, trying to overhear their interaction.

"So today's been kinda crazy," Zane observed.

"Tell me about it," Hadley said.

Okay, that's fine. . . . Keep it up. . . . Keep it up. . . .

"You feeling better?"

"Me? Yeah. I'm fine, totally fine." *The lady doth protest too much, methinks,* I thought.

"It just wasn't like you to drop the ball in English class today like that."

"It was uncharacteristic and I apologize—"

"Hey, no need to apologize, I'm just sayin'."

"Sayin' what?"

Zane stared mutely and I had to do something. I couldn't let Ms. Pitt single-handedly destroy this mood! I nudged her ever so slightly in the back with my elbow and nonchalantly turned. She gave a little look over her shoulder and pivoted to face Zane again.

"Just . . . you know . . . just makin' sure you're okay, that's all."

I gave a sly smile to Hadley and very coyly (seriously, maybe I should be a spy or something, I was feeling increasingly stealth) gestured with my head to keep it going. Hadley flashed him a big grin. "Thank you. I am fine now. And I appreciate your concern."

"So . . . kinda cool with the dance on a Monday and the Candy-Grams and all," he said.

"Yes."

Mr. Hudson appeared at the doorway of the cafeteria and was scanning the room. I knew I now had my excuse to get much closer to Zane and Hadley without looking like a complete loon and I made a beeline for him. The high heels click-clicked on the cafeteria floor and I saw Mr. Hudson notice me approach. He did an adorable double take, obviously approving of my wardrobe and general style update. . . . I knew getting Ms. Pitt out of her drab garb and into something edgier would be appreciated. Already it was clearly paying off.

"Whoa, you look—" Mr. Hudson said.

"Let's dance," I cut in and dragged Mr. Hudson out onto the dance floor. He was taken aback but (I'd say) secretly thrilled as I directed him squarely next to Zane and me. I just had to hear what was up!

I put my arms around Mr. Hudson's neck and made sure there was a good amount of space in between us. There would be no hanky-panky teacher action on *my* watch. He smiled at me.

"I wanted to tell you how lovely you look tonight," Mr. Hudson said.

I strained to hear Zane and Hadley's conversation and wasn't exactly paying attention to Mr. Hudson. "Come again?"

"I said . . . you look lovely," he repeated.

"Oh, thanks, thanks. Enough with the granola-wear, right?" I smiled and continued to eavesdrop.

"Wait, what did you just say again?" I heard Hadley ask.

Yeah, what was it?! I thought to myself desperately.

"I said . . . I sent the Candy-Gram. I'm your secret admirer," said Zane.

"Shut! Up!" I squealed in response, and everyone shot confused eyes my way to make sure that was actually Ms. Pitt screaming like a way-too-spirited cheerleader.

"And I guess it's not so secret anymore. . . ." Zane whispered, and edged a bit away from me in Ms. Pitt's body, trying to give Hadley and him some privacy.

But Zane, don't you see?! I'm right here!

I couldn't miss this and tried to direct Mr. Hudson back in their direction—*Zane Henderson sent me a secret admirer Candy-Gram!!*

"Why, what a lovely thing to do, Zane. Thank you for sending me a Candy-Gram," Hadley said.

Lovely thing to do? No! No! No! I thought, panicky. He didn't deliver a bag of potatoes or help mend a fence—he got me a Candy-Gram! Let's see some excitement!

"Yeah, I was a little nervous about sending it," Zane admitted.

I was craning my neck, desperate to overhear this exchange—this was one of the most thrilling things that had ever happened to me . . . and I wasn't even ME!

"Mr. Wells was looking for you earlier," Mr. Hudson told me. What Mr. Hudson failed to grasp was that Mr. Wells paled on the excitement Richter scale compared to this dance moment!

"Huh," I responded dismissively, craning my neck to keep tabs on Zane.

"Is something wrong with your neck?" Mr. Hudson asked.

"No. Why?" I asked, realizing as I said it I *was* straining my neck to hear. I probably looked like a turtle stretching out of my shell. I tried to act more normal. "Oh, yeah, little crick or something."

Zane and Hadley were drifting too far away—it was nearly impossible to hear them. I desperately tried to steer me and Mr. Hudson back in their direction. The effect was probably more than a bit psychotic.

"You know, I've always had a . . . well, a thing for you, Hadley," Zane said, despite his crimson face and obvious discomfort sharing this information.

No way! Zane has a thing for me?!

"I guess it probably doesn't come as a shock to know that I've always had a thing for you, Carol," Mr. Hudson said a bit awkwardly. I knew I should say something but he would just have to wait.

Ms. Pitt clearly knew how much this would mean to me and she responded fairly normally with genuine sincerity. "That is really good to hear, Zane. Because I believe I've always had a thing for you, too," she said. I could tell Ms. Pitt probably felt very nearly creepy saying this to a student but I so appreciated it!

Zane brightened. "Really?"

"I'm fairly certain, yes," Hadley responded.

"So . . . aren't you going to respond?" Mr. Hudson pleaded. But I was way checked out and swooning over this Zane exchange!

My stomach was doing cartwheels!

"Oh yeah. That's cool," I said a bit dismissively to Mr. Hudson. Then I realized this could possibly be just as important to Ms. Pitt as Zane was to me. I had to at least *try* to focus.

I turned to Mr. Hudson and looked him dead in the eye. "Really, Mr. Hudson—"

"Randy."

"Randy. I'm happy to hear that. It's about time I went out and had some sort of a social life," I said, and Hadley flipped around and glared, overhearing that! Well, it was true—Ms. Pitt *should* date.

Mr. Hudson's face brightened. "So then . . . would you like to go out? This Saturday maybe?"

Zane was looking longingly at Hadley, searching her face. He was definitely inching toward her and Ms. Pitt knew that boys just don't lean in toward girls unless there's one goal and one goal alone. . . .

Zane was moving in to KISS her!

"Uh . . . Carol?" Mr. Hudson asked me again. But hello—I was just a little bit more focused on my *first kiss*!

"OHMYGOD!" I squealed at the horror show unrolling before my eyes! Ms. Pitt can't get to experience MY first kiss!

And the gods responded as Ms. Pitt averted this and turned Hadley's face JUST in the nick of time so that Zane's lips missed her cheek! I took shallow breaths as if I had narrowly avoided a natural disaster.

"Carol?" Mr. Hudson asked yet again, his deepening uncertainty coloring his voice.

I had to snap out of it and address Mr. Hudson. "Sure! Cool! I mean I'd love to." I barely got all that out when Hadley linked arms in my own and dragged me off.

CHAPTER 19

The real Ms. Pitt and I finally found an area to talk, occupied only by a clandestine making-out couple, who were clearly oblivious of our arrival. We waited a second and shared an exasperated look. This couple was NOT coming up for air.

"Do you mind?" I asked sarcastically.

Finally the couple pulled out of their lip lock and were startled to see Ms. Pitt glowering at them. "Sorry, Ms. P!" the boy said, and yanked his girlfriend off with the charm of a caveman.

Out of nowhere Mr. Wells snuck up—he was like a shark, moving silently and with obvious intent to maim.

"I see you chose to overlook the students clearly violating code 5.24, which states that teachers must give detention to any couple on school property engaging in affectionate acts such as kissing—"

"But aren't *you* the principal? Shouldn't you stop

them, then?" Hadley asked with conviction.

Mr. Wells was silenced. "I will address them in due time. Now then, Ms. Pitt. I have been looking for you all evening."

"Can we talk at another time? I'm sort of in the middle of something here," I said. (Important things like *nearly getting kissed by Zane Henderson*!) But the minute I said it, I was sure Mr. Wells was *not* used to Ms. Pitt being so flippant with him.

"Let me guess. Your students come first?"

Hadley stepped forward and wanted to backpedal this tension. "Mr. Wells, with all due respect . . . I want to assure you that today's interview—and I'm sure for all of its . . . strangeness—"

"'Strangeness' does not begin to describe it," said Mr. Wells curtly.

"Let me assure you today was . . . well, far from ideal and completely situational. And I am—I mean, Ms. Pitt—is totally capable of chairing the English department. As a student of hers, I can attest to her skill," Hadley said.

Hadley locked eyes with me and silently pleaded to take this seriously. "Mr. Wells, I realize it may be too late," I said. "But there is nothing more that I aspire to and I'd do an exceptional job as chair of the English department." Now, that sounded official.

I could tell Hadley was nearly vibrating with dread . . . and it probably *was* too late for her dream appointment. We sat there in loaded silence.

"It's not too late, Ms. Pitt," Mr. Wells said with serious reluctance in his voice.

"It's not?!" Both Hadley and I chimed in together.

"No. Truth of the matter is, you *are* a devoted teacher, Ms. Pitt. And that has not gone unnoticed," he said.

"Thanks!" Hadley chirped too enthusiastically. "But . . . what about during the interview when I *prematurely,* well—" She fumbled for the word.

"Blazed. Didn't that hurt my chances?" I said.

"The board saw that as more evidence of your devotion. Leaving prematurely for the sake of a student only highlighted that conviction." He paused. "Even I was moved by that display."

"You?" I had to ask.

"Yes, Ms. Pitt. Congratulations. The board would like to extend an offer to chair the English department."

Hadley leaped into the air with elated buoyancy. "Woo-hooo!"

Mr. Wells eyed Hadley a bit suspiciously again.

"See? Students love me!" I tried to explain Hadley's outburst, and he responded with a half smile. "Thank you, Mr. Wells."

"I knew you'd want to know immediately." He shook my hand.

"Congratulations, Ms. Pitt. You did it." With that, Mr. Wells strolled off, and Hadley and I burst into a spontaneous hug. And let me tell you, it is beyond weird to hug yourself!

"I am so psyched for you!" I said.

"And if we could just switch our bodies back, I could get a whole lot more excited about the whole situation," joked Hadley. And with the reintroduction of the whole body-switch topic, we felt our spirits deflate a bit.

"Oh, yeah. There's that."

"Yup," I responded. "There's still that. It doesn't look like we're switching back anytime soon, does it."

"No. But you shouldn't get too down. Zane Henderson did just try to kiss *you*," Hadley said. "And now you must know for sure that that boy is so into you. . . ."

"He does actually like *me*, huh?"

"He does. Not Tatum. *You*." She paused and smiled at me as I soaked in this realization.

"And Mr. Hudson has got it bad for you, whoa, nelly," I said. "He asked you on a date, FYI, and I accepted. . . ."

"So today I got my dream job *and* a date!" Hadley said. "Okay, this has been the freakiest day. . . ."

"You deserve everything."

"And so do you."

"You know," I said, "if I ever get back into my own lackluster, flat-as-a-pancake body, I will kiss the ground I walk on and celebrate every rainbow and sunset and moment of life. I swear. I promise to do more with my life than study!"

"Yeah. Like kissing Zane Henderson!" Hadley teased, and I fist-bumped her in the arm.

"And you have to make time for snuggling up to Mr. Hudson, missy," I ribbed back.

She hit me back in the arm playfully. "That's Randy, thank you very much. . . ."

"Right, *Randy*."

"Let's be honest—we both need more balance in our lives," Hadley said. "And I cannot believe I am saying this to a student—but you need to study less, lady. Get your nose out of that book and *live*!"

I looked her dead in the eye. "And I could say the same to you."

Suddenly Hadley looked up to the sky as if addressing the gods. "I know. And if anyone's up there listening, I swear I'll do it! I'll volunteer for *fewer* school activities but I'll give *more* of my actual self. I'll give my students a less scattered and a more plugged-in, *happier* version of me!

Just let me switch back and chair that English department in my regular old body and you'll see."

"We have learned a lot," I said.

"We have. And what was it that we said earlier this morning?" Hadley asked.

"'Ohmygod, ohmygod, this is not possible!'" I joked.

"No, no. The quote we read from *To Kill a Mockingbird*. About seeing something from someone else's perspective," Hadley stated.

It dawned on me Ms. Pitt was right—school wasn't just about grades, it was about *learning*. And I don't think I truly grasped that lesson *or* what the book was actually about until this very moment. Sure, I had read *To Kill a Mockingbird* and studied the vocab words. (And look where *that* got me.) I didn't study it to absorb or truly understand its meaning. But now I completely *got* the message. I *had* seen things from a different perspective today. And what a world of difference it had made.

I locked eyes with Ms. Pitt and said, "You mean the part about '*you never really understand a person until you consider things from his point of view—*'"

"'*Until you climb—*'" Ms. Pitt added.

Together we grinned at each other and both said: "'*—into his skin and walk around in it.*'"

At that moment, the lights of the cafeteria CRASHED and SPARKED. Flickers of electricity lit up the darkened cafeteria like the Fourth of July and floated down to the dance floor. Students screamed and the room plunged into darkness.

Within a few moments, the lights resumed and students hugged one another, grasping for reassurance.

"Okay, that was beyond freaky," I said, and as I spoke I realized—

I JUST HEARD MY VOICE! NOT MS. PITT'S VOICE, BUT MY VOICE!

Ms. Pitt let out a delighted squeal and patted down her womanly boobs for reassurance. Yup—she *wasn't* flat as a pancake anymore and those were definitely her breasts!

"Hadley, do you know what this means?!" Ms. Pitt trumpeted, eyes glowing with giddy excitement and relief.

"Yipppeeee!" I squealed with the craziness of a kid who has just plowed through their entire Halloween loot in one sitting. I felt deranged . . . deluded . . . and delighted! Relief flooded and coursed through my body—my body, Hadley Della Fox's glorious, teenage, wondrous gift of a body!

Ms. Pitt and I locked arms and we twirled about merrily, circling the room and giddily laughing together. The whole insanity of the day and the sheer relief flooded our every step. Truth be told, we probably looked a wee bit shnockered.

I stopped on the dance floor and we looked into each other's eyes, soaking in the details of each other's face—and this time, I was looking at Ms. Pitt, not at myself!

I clung to Ms. Pitt with everything I had—and I had never been so happy to see her before in my entire life! Tears flooded my eyes and crazed laughs kept erupting from us both.

"Hey! Save it for the slow dance!" Someone yelled from the sidelines, obviously commenting on our hug-fest on the cafeteria floor. Laughter erupted and we both joined in.

Mr. Hudson placed a gentle hand on Ms. Pitt's shoulder and she turned, flashing a megawatt smile. "Are you okay?" he asked sweetly.

Ms. Pitt locked eyes with me and smiled warmly. "No, I'm better than okay! I'm fantastic!" She beamed.

"Me, too," I gushed, feeling an elation course through my body that I had never known before. "And maybe . . . just maybe . . . I'm even fabulous."

Zane walked up and overheard my last comment and chimed in, "Tell me something I don't know."

I turned around and lobbed a huge smile to adorable Zane. "And you know something?" I asked him.

"What's that?" he responded, matching me in the smile department.

"I used to hate Mondays."

"And now?" Ms. Pitt asked.

"I'd say Mondays pretty much rock." The four of us laughed and luxuriated in the warmth and I realized I had never, ever been so thrilled to be myself, exactly as I am.

"Yup." Zane grinned. He leaned over and whispered into my ear, "Best Monday I've had in a while." I swear I felt my toes curl back into my feet. I didn't realize I was the sort of person who could swoon, but apparently I was highly swoon-capable. It was a good thing for a teenage girl to find out about herself.

"Though I could think of something that this Monday *is* missing," Zane whispered with pepperminty breath, not substandard-typical-teenage-boy-woeful-hygiene breath. I had to steady myself.

"Oh, yeah?" My face nearly hurt I was smiling so huge.

"That kiss from before. It was, uh . . . cut short." Zane was bright red and his smile was equally huge.

"What a shame," I heard myself say, and I was *so* pleased. I sounded like a real *flirty* teenager! One that went to the mall, one who *didn't* just read textbooks and obsessively worry about getting into Stanford at age thirteen! One who had, you know—*a life*!

"We should correct that," Zane said, and I giggled, covering my mouth shyly—jeez, that teenage giggle stuff was instinctive, too!

I locked eyes with Ms. Pitt and grinned. She was no dummy and seemed plugged into this teenage experience; she knew *exactly* what was going on here.

The familiar opening chords of Savage Garden's "Truly Madly Deeply" started up. It was a song that Soup, Nan, and I just loved to make fun of. It was drippy, predictable, and had sort of lame lyrics. It was also the sort of song that you secretly turn up and sing really loud when you were alone. (But you'd never admit that in public.)

"Care to dance again?" Zane asked.

"Why not?"

Zane took my hand and I hoped it wasn't a clammy disaster. I also made sure I steered him close enough to Soup and Nan so that I could keep tabs on them.

"Join me on the dance floor?" I heard Mr. Hudson ask Ms. Pitt. I turned around long enough to see her nod yes. And her smile had a positively un-thirty-two-year-old beam and was a *bit* more teenage. Success! Mr. Hudson and Ms. Pitt followed us out onto the dance floor.

So there we were—Mr. Hudson and Ms. Pitt and Zane

and myself all slow-dancing under the twinkly lights of Burroughs Junior High cafeteria. It was positively too much, entirely freaky, and completely *fabulous*.

"So . . . how about that kiss, then?" Zane asked softly.

He smiled down at me, his face blushing and his eyes sparkling with affection.

Yup. It was pretty much the greatest Monday. Ever.

ACKNOWLEDGMENTS

The authors would like to send a big bouquet of thanks to the following readers for their terrific responses and insightful comments on the manuscript: Sonya Caputo-Cole; Rachel Martel; Isabel Sebbane; and Gracie Lawrence, Alison Kaplon, Miranda Wilkins, and Kheyana McKie, middle-school students at the Dalton School in New York, as well as their dynamite librarian, Roxanne Hsu Feldman.

Heather Hach adds: "I have to thank Brenda Bowen, my brilliant editor, for steering this book into its rightful harbor. Also, thank you to Mary Rodgers for extending the opportunity to do this in the first place and to my literary agent, Richard Abate, for seeing it through. A big shout-out is necessary for my adorable and supportive husband, Jason Hearne, who never tires of me sneaking off to the computer for one more peck at the keyboard. I could not do it without him or without my parents, Bruce and Muriel Hach, who are deliriously devoted and have always fostered my creativity—thank you!"